Praise for Donald J. Trump

"I'm intelligent. Some people would say I'm very, very, very intelligent."

—Donald J. Trump, in *Fortune*

"I love beautiful women, and beautiful women love me."

—Donald J. Trump, speaking to Norwegian talk show host Fredrik Skavlan

"It is very hard for them to attack me on looks, because I am so good-looking."

—Donald J. Trump, on NBC's *Meet the Press*, August 7, 2015

"What a great honor it must be for you to honor me tonight."

—Donald J. Trump, at his Comedy Central Roast

"I could stand in the middle of Fifth Avenue and shoot somebody, and I wouldn't lose any voters, okay? It's, like, incredible."

—Donald J. Trump, speaking at a rally in Sioux Center, January 23, 2016

"The show is 'Trump.' And it is sold-out performances everywhere."

—Donald J. Trump, in *Playboy*, March 1990

"We want to see winning. We want to see win, win, win— constant winning. And you'll say—if I'm president . . . 'Please,

Mr. President, we're winning too much. We can't stand it anymore. Can't we have a loss?' And I'll say no, we're going to keep winning, winning, winning."

—Donald J. Trump, speaking at
Liberty University, January 2016

THE DAY OF
THE DONALD

ANDREW SHAFFER

THE DAY OF THE DONALD

TRUMP TRUMPS AMERICA!

CROOKED
LANE

NEW YORK

Copyright © 2016 by Quick Brown Fox & Company LLC.

Published in the United States by Crooked Lane Books, an imprint of The Quick Brown Fox & Company LLC.

Crooked Lane Books and its logo are trademarks of The Quick Brown Fox & Company LLC.

Library of Congress Catalog-in-Publication data available upon request.

ISBN (paperback): 978-1-68331-045-7
ISBN (ePub): 978-1-68331-046-4
ISBN (Kindle): 978-1-68331-047-1
ISBN (ePDF): 978-1-68331-048-8

Cover design by Louis Malcangi
Cover illustration by Bruce Emmett
Book design by Jennifer Canzone

Printed in the United States.

www.crookedlanebooks.com

Crooked Lane Books
34 West 27th St., 10th Floor
New York, NY 10001

First Edition: June 2016

10 9 8 7 6 5 4 3 2 1

"It's like Mahatma Gandhi said: First they ignore you, then they laugh at you, then they fight you, then you win . . . and then you make them all kiss your ass."
—President-Elect Trump in his acceptance speech,
November 8, 2016

THE DAY OF THE DONALD

PROLOGUE

★ ★ ★ ★

JANUARY 20, 2017

The skies were overcast on a bitterly cold January day, but that didn't stop the massive crowd from gathering at the US Capitol Building. The crowd was bundled up, pumped up, and in more than a few cases, liquored up. This was a day that would set the Guinness World Record for the most fistfights at one location in a single day.

But far away from the protests, up on the Capitol steps, a thin ray of sunshine broke through the clouds to illuminate what, from a distance, looked like a thick wisp of rust-flavored cotton candy. The strings blew about in the wind, eventually settling back down on top of the head of the man about to become the forty-fifth president of the United States—Donald J. Trump.

The billionaire businessman and WWE Hall of Famer stood tall and proud on the platform, joined by his five children. No first lady. The "October Surprise" of this election cycle had been his split from Melania—which did nothing to slow his momentum. If anything, polls indicated it may have helped.

As five Cessnas flew overhead in tight formation, Donald Trump stepped forward. He placed his hand on the Bible being held by Donald Trump Jr., which was in turn resting atop a copy of *Trump: The Art of the Deal*. He raised his right hand as Chief Justice Roberts administered the oath of office.

After being sworn in, Trump stepped to the microphone.

"My fellow Americans, we are about to do some really, really fantastic things! It's gonna be terrific! It's a new day. Last November, the American people made their voices heard loud and clear in nearly every state. California, Illinois, I don't know what you were thinking—you got some big financial problems going on out there, and I'm a very good businessman. I could have helped out, I'm just saying.

"And now we're going to Make! America! Great! Again! That's right. If you don't have a hat, by the way, they're selling them at the merch booths near the exits. Twenty-five dollars for some really good workmanship. It's quality, a great value.

"This is a terrific nation. Sure, it has some problems. But hey—I have a lot of experience inheriting extravagant commodities, and they almost always retain most of their value. I totally got this.

"Let's stop to give a great round of applause to Obama. I was tough on him during the campaign, but he did a pretty nice job for a Hawaiian American."

The viewers at home saw a shot of President Obama waving graciously to Trump and the crowd. And then, perhaps thinking the cameras had already cut away, Obama turned to Michelle and mouthed, "We can go." The outgoing first couple were halfway out of their seats by the time the cameras returned to Trump.

"I want to say how humbled I am to have earned this sacred trust. I *want* to say that, but we all know I completely deserve this. I'm the most qualified guy to win the presidency since

Eisenhower. So let me say to you: Good choice, America. You nailed this one.

"Let's make America great again, from sea to shiny sea. It's not just for rich-o's, either. Look, folks, my car has windows. I know that there're some run-down neighborhoods in America. We're going to fix that. The poor people are going to be so happy. I promise tomorrow, day one, to end the program that gives tax breaks for making your home more energy efficient. We're going to replace it with tax breaks for making your home more classy. I want a granite countertop in every kitchen and Bermuda grass on every lawn!

"So, America, here's what I'm gonna do. I'm going to be a first-rate, grade-A, big-league commander in chief. I'm going to deliver the goods. That's what you gotta do, right? Deliver the goods. I'm great at delivering the goods. There's nobody better. We're going to turn a profit in every sense of the word. And we're going to tell America's enemies . . . you're fired!"

There was a two-minute-long wait for the applause to subside. Half a mile away, a car was flipped over, set on fire, and then flipped over while on fire—all for still having a Bernie bumper sticker.

In Madison, Wisconsin, a frat boy passed out. He'd been playing a drinking game where he took a shot every time Trump said the word "great." He would survive. The new president would even cover the cost to pump his stomach.

And in Manhattan, six late-night talk show hosts joined hands in a prayer circle and gave thanks for the bounty that they were about to receive.

"As the great Abraham Lincoln once said, 'Put up or shut up.' And I am the best at putting up. I put up Trump Tower. I put up the Trump casino. I put up the other Trump Tower in Chicago, and have you seen how tall it is? Majestic. It is a building that Abraham Lincoln would have been thrilled by if he had lived to see it. He'd be amazed. It would have blown his mind."

He paused as if he'd just realized his poor choice of words but continued on. Such was the Trump way.

"I'm a rising tide, America, and I'm going to lift all the boats. If you don't have a boat, you'll be able to afford one by the time I'm done."

Trump paused for dramatic effect. He brushed away a tear, or maybe his eye just itched.

"We're going to do more than make America great. America is going to be really, truly amazing. This is the finest, richest, most upscale nation in the world. I'm proud to have my name on it, I really am.

"God bless America, and let's make some money."

He waved to the cheering masses and headed inside, out of the cold.

The Trump era had begun.

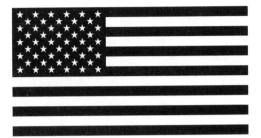

Eighteen Months Later

CHAPTER ONE

⭐ ⭐ ⭐ ⭐

THE EVEN GREATER WALL

Jimmie Bernwood didn't know what was more suffocating: the darkness or the stale air. How far below the surface were they now? Forty, fifty feet? As long as the concrete-reinforced tunnel didn't collapse, he supposed it didn't much matter.

Jimmie heard a cough behind him. A deep, phlegmy cough. The old man. The moment he'd seen the man's sunken face and withered body in the back of the Toyota, he'd pegged him as a goner. Unfit to army-crawl underneath a limbo stick, let alone the mile and a half of tunnel leading to the promised land. Yet here they were, nearly at the end of their journey, and the old man was still breathing. For how much longer, Jimmie couldn't say.

Sad truth was, the old man wasn't his problem. Jimmie was simply a journalist on the trail of a story. Once the migrants set foot on the other side of the Even Greater Wall, he would watch as they stumbled off into the desert. He'd take a drink of water from his canteen. Slip back into the tunnel. Repeat the trek a few more times—as many times as it took to get the story. As many times as it took to get inside the heads of the men and women desperate enough to make the dangerous journey. All any of them wanted was a better life. Was that a

3

crime? In the immortal words of Secretary of the Energies Palin, "You betcha."

Something crunched beneath Jimmie's forearm. Lots of scorpions and tarantulas down here. Whatever it was, he brushed its crumpled body aside and crawled on. He'd been stung and bitten more times than he could count. His bare arms were as mottled with scabs as a fry cook's.

What you really had to look out for down here were the bigger pests. Run headfirst into a pack of hungry rats, and say hello to heaven. There was no room to turn around; they'd eat you alive.

Another cough. Even if the old man survived the coming days and nights crossing the no-man's-land, he wasn't going to get a job picking fruit. Not in the condition he was in. The last thing anyone hiring migrants wanted to deal with was body disposal. Though they might just let him lie there in the orange grove to fertilize the plants.

Up ahead, he could see a faint sliver of light. The edge of the tarp that covered the opening let a shaft of moonlight through—not much, but just enough. The end was in sight.

Twenty-five minutes later, Jimmie Bernwood was throwing the tarp open and gulping down his first breath of fresh air in hours. Fresh, unpolluted air. It smelled like jobs. Like health care. Like hope.

Thirty-six minutes after that, he was helping the last of the American migrants to their feet in Mexico.

And ten seconds after *that*, he was staring into a bright light, straight down the barrel of an AR-15.

CHAPTER TWO

✮ ✮ ✮ ✮

SHAWSHANK
(MINUS THE REDEMPTION)

After the Mexican border agents lowered their guns but before they could cuff him, Jimmie pulled out his duct-taped wallet.

"I have rights," he said, fishing out his press credentials. "Don't you believe in freedom of the press down here?"

A helicopter buzzed overhead as the agents examined his 2009 Cannes Film Festival press pass.

Jimmie shielded his eyes from their spotlights. "They don't hand those out to just anyone. You have to be a member of an elite media organization to be on the red carpet at Cannes. That year, I interviewed Harrison Ford and Natalie Portman."

This piqued the interest of one of the agents. "*¿Harrison Ford?*"

"Han Solo," Jimmie said, pointing at the press pass. Although his days on red carpets were long gone, the Mexican border patrol didn't need to know that.

"*Han Solo,*" the agent repeated, staring for another moment at the press pass. He shook his head and handed it back to Jimmie. "*No eres Han Solo. Te ves como . . . Chewbacca.*"

This got a few chuckles from the other agents. With the crazy beard and unkempt hair, Jimmie had to admit he probably did look a little like a Wookiee. His postbreakup "no-shave November" scruff had eventually given way to a "zero-fucks-given 2017" beard. He was pretty sure it was 2018 now. Like, 90 percent sure.

The agents weren't really interested in hearing a sob story. They carted Jimmie and the American migrants off to San Miguel—the most lawless prison this side of Guantanamo. No phone call. No text. Not even a tweet. "I want my hundred and forty characters!" Jimmie shouted as they tossed him into the general population.

The Mexican authorities no doubt expected him to be shivved and left to bleed out in the shower. If so, they had no idea just how resourceful Jimmie Bernwood was.

On his first day on the inside, he would seek out the baddest *hijo de puta* in the yard . . . and beg him for protection. In exchange, he would use his superior command of the written word to pen love letters to the man's girlfriend or wife.

Unfortunately, Jimmie quickly learned he wasn't the only aspiring Nicholas Sparks in San Miguel. The prison love-letter racket was every bit as competitive as New York City publishing. Too many pencil jockeys. Not enough horses. The big difference between New York and San Miguel, however, was that if you scored a cover story for *Rolling Stone*, your competition wasn't going to shank you in retaliation.

Anyway, that's how Jimmie came to be shivved and left to bleed out in the shower.

CHAPTER THREE

★ ★ ★ ★

HELLO, NURSE

Jimmie woke in a hospital bed. An IV drip was feeding into his right arm. Based on the fuzzy feeling in his head, he was being drugged. No casts on his arms or legs, though, so he hadn't been broken too bad in the prison attack. If this were a movie, Jimmie would rip the needle out and stagger off into the night. Unfortunately, the handcuffs on both his wrists put a damper on any escape plans.

A television mounted on the far wall was tuned to an English-language station—MSNBC, according to the scroller. They cut from a commercial for Trump Cola straight to video of a Trump rally.

A banner across the stage read, "AMERICA IS GREAT AGAIN." So did most of the red hats in the crowd, Jimmie assumed. The crowd was hanging on Trump's every word, even though he was probably twenty minutes into his third massive digression of the afternoon. They'd paid two large for these tickets, and by gosh, they were going to enjoy them.

"Prince Charles? That guy's a boob. Total. Boob. Let me tell you something, folks, all of England's princes and princesses together don't add up to one of our princesses at Disney. Not even close. You want to see some real princesses? How about the USA Freedom Girls for America?"

Trump exited to thundering applause as the dance team took the stage to perform their new single. Not their strongest. Jimmie thought about changing the channel, but nobody'd left him the remote.

Trump returned for an encore and launched straight into his List of Enemies (always a crowd pleaser). The audience shouted along with the president: "Hillary! Hollywood! Pelosi! Rowling!"

Trump raised his hand for quiet. As had become the custom, the crowd all raised their hands back at him, also calling for quiet.

"You've been great today, West Virginia! This is my favorite of the Virginias. Let me tell you, America is close to being the greatest it's ever been. It really, truly is, folks. You know this. We have the greatest people, the greatest cities. We have all the greatest freedoms . . ."

"EXCEPT FREEDOM OF RELIGION!" a lone voice shouted, loud enough to be picked up by MSNBC's microphones.

Heads swiveled to stare at a woman who had ripped off her Trump shirt to reveal her true colors: Underneath, she was wearing a Bernie shirt—the one with the golden house finch, which was somehow appearing on more and more bootleg merchandise even after being banned on Etsy.

A shocked murmur rumbled through the crowd. *A protester? Here?!* The protests at Trump's rallies had dwindled to almost zero once he'd started handing out free bike chains. Now this woman's sudden appearance created the same reactions a cockroach would. Most people were getting as far away as possible, while a few rushed toward her, eagerly awaiting their chance to stomp on something.

"Equal treatment for Kardashians! Let them in! Let them in! Let them—"

The woman's chanting was abruptly cut off when a man who looked like a middle school social studies teacher backhanded her across the mouth. Then the man balled his hand into a fist and punched her square in the face, garnering applause from the crowd and knocking the woman to the pavement.

"Okay, okay, that's enough," said Trump from the podium. "No more of that. What have I told you? Two punches is plenty for a broad. Let her up."

The crowd obediently pulled the protestor to her feet, even though it had technically been one punch and one slap.

"Okay, look, lady. I don't know what it is that sent you on the warpath—though we can guess, it's probably cramps," said Trump, drawing a huge roar of laughter. The danger had passed; they were having fun again.

"But you need to understand, I love the freedom of religion. It's one of the five top freedoms. Those Kardashians can be any religion they want. But if it's a religion that wants to blow us up, they don't get to come here. Anybody is welcome in America—they just have to change to a religion that doesn't want to blow us up. I don't think that's too much to ask."

As the crowd cheered, several security personnel appeared, each holding an oversized American flag. With swift, practiced movements, they wrapped the flags around the protestor before pinning her arms and legs, then covering her completely. They lifted her on their shoulders like a roll of American-flag carpet and carried her out of the arena.

"Husbands, this is what happens when you don't give your wives enough attention," Trump said. "Be good to them. Even if they're as ugly as that one."

The station cut to the in-studio host, Lena Dunham. She rolled her eyes so hard that Jimmie worried she might have been having a seizure. "That was the president, speaking at a rally promoting his new program retraining out-of-work coal miners as golf caddies—"

The TV went black. Jimmie glanced around the room. He spied a dark-haired woman in a sharp, navy-blue blazer pointing a remote at the television. Her matching skirt only made it to midthigh, giving him a not-unpleasing view of her long legs.

She spun around in one fluid motion, like she'd reached the end of a catwalk. "Look who's done napping," she said with a polished British accent. "Think you can stay awake this time?"

"Do we know each other?" Jimmie asked. He doubted they'd met—he would have remembered those legs.

"You've been in and out of consciousness for over seventy-two hours. This is the third time we've had this conversation."

"Sorry about that."

"That's the third time you've apologized as well," she said. "You're nothing if not consistent."

"First time I've ever heard that."

The woman said, "Third time." She paused. "Anyway, since I don't have all day, here's the pitch: My name is Emma Blythe. I'm with the White House."

"You're a Brit in the White House? Not a Prince Charles sympathizer, then?"

She smiled a patient, thin-lipped smile and continued. "I'm here to extend you an offer of employment as a ghostwriter."

He'd never tried his hand at ghostwriting before. Hadn't even attempted a book-length manuscript, outside of an abandoned novel or two. Or five. Okay, nine, but who was counting? Point was, she'd mistaken him for someone else.

"Too bad you came all this way," he said. "Doesn't sound like my sort of thing. And even if I was into ghostwriting, I couldn't care less about politics. But I've already told you this."

She nodded. "You're not interested in politics, but you are interested in writing about the American migrant experience for *Cigar Aficionado* magazine. Strange, isn't it?"

"Apparently their readers enjoy chomping on stogies while reading about poor, unemployed people crawling around in the dirt," Jimmie said. "It's just a paycheck."

"What are they paying you?"

He told her the number, which wasn't much.

"Here's what we can offer you," she said, quoting a number four times as large. Maybe five times—his math wasn't super.

"For the entire project? Do I get, like, half now, half later?"

"That would be your salary. Per week. And to answer your next question, you would be ghostwriting the president's memoir."

"The president of . . ."

"The United States."

"You want me to help write the autobiography . . . of Donald Trump?"

11

CHAPTER FOUR

★ ★ ★ ★

AN OFFER YOU CAN'T REFUSE

"**T**here are dozens of Trump biographies on the shelves," Emma said. "Even before he was elected president, the American people were fascinated with him. Half of the books about him are full of shit."

"And the rest?" Jimmie asked.

"Are only half full of shit. Those are the ones he wrote himself."

Jimmie laughed and immediately regretted it. Not just because he felt a sharp pain in his abs, but also because this woman clearly wasn't joking.

"He doesn't want another cookie-cutter biography," Emma said. "He wants to write a memoir of his time in office. The working title is *America's Greatest Decade*."

"Decade?"

"He'll have to remove term limits, but he considers that a formality."

"Still, sounds a little optimistic."

"He could wait to write the book until after his term, but he doesn't know when that will be. He's afraid he's going to miss the yacht," she said. "Besides, he wants it on shelves during his reelection campaign. He wants to tout all he's done for the country. Discharging our debt to China, the buyout of Cuba, the program to put chandeliers in every classroom in the country."

Jimmie felt his cheeks flush. "And my name was the first that came to mind."

"Let's just say you weren't too far down the list. He's a big fan of your work. You'll be given total access. You can follow him into the bathroom if you want to." She paused. "He actually specifically asked me to mention that to you. That he has nothing to hide in that department."

That message delivered, her tone brightened: "He wants to come across as open and honest. You won't be asked to sugarcoat anything. No restrictions. I know this is a lot to take in," she said. "But I'm going to need an answer before I leave."

"When are you leaving?"

"I need to catch my flight in an hour and thirty-seven minutes. Which means you have five minutes to decide, James." She glanced at her phone. "Four minutes."

Although Jimmie had never heard from the president before, it made perfect sense that Trump was a fan of his. Jimmie had been the one whose reporting had forced Ted Cruz out of the race. It was right when Cruz was preparing his all-out "This time we'll *really* stop him" surprise reactivation of his campaign a week before the Republican National Convention. The story had also cost Jimmie his career. There was the lawsuit brought by SeaWorld against the *Daily Blabber*. The jury trial, where Jimmie's ethics were called into question. The $180 million verdict. The appeal. The upheld verdict.

After that, his name was poison. No disreputable blog would have him, and he had no interest in working for the reputable ones.

The assignment for *Cigar Aficionado* had come about through an old editor who still tossed him a freelance gig from time to time.

So while his past was painful, his present wasn't exactly all kittens and rainbows. And this opportunity was almost too good to be true. Forget crawling around in the dirt—he'd be working in the White House. Or, as some of the administration's critics called it, the "Gold House." (Trump took this as a tremendous compliment.) What interested Jimmie more than the steady work, however, was the opportunity to see his ex-girlfriend again—Cat Diaz. What would she say if she saw him palling around with the president?

"Is Cat Diaz still working there in the press corps?" Jimmie asked.

"She was your boss at the *Daily Blabber*, wasn't she? Fired you, right? If it's going to be a problem for you to work together, we can revoke her credentials."

"That won't be necessary," he said. "Do you know if she's still seeing that reporter from the *Times*? Lester Dorset. Always flashing that Pulitzer of his around like he won the Super Bowl."

"I don't keep up with the latest gossip," Emma said. "Isn't that your specialty?"

Jimmie didn't say anything.

Emma looked at her phone. "Time's up. What'll it be? Ready to return home?"

Jimmie grunted.

"So is that disgusting noise a yes? I really need to be on my way."

"What's the alternative, again?"

"I think you know that."

"Because you've told me before?"

"Because you're not as stupid as you pretend to be. If I leave you here, you'll be thrown back into San Miguel after you're healed. Imagine what will happen to you after a month. After a year." She paused. "After *ten years*."

In another decade, Jimmie would be in his forties. A decade after that, his fifties. Was there anything after that? He thought back to the old man coughing in the tunnel, the old man who was going to die in San Miguel. How many of the migrants would kill for the opportunity Jimmie was being handed?

He would accept the job. For that old man and for every migrant who had ever dreamed of a better life and fallen short.

He'd accept it primarily to avoid returning to jail, of course.

Secondly, for a chance to show up his ex.

Thirdly, for the steady paycheck.

But fourthly, for those poor souls who hadn't been blessed with the talent to turn prose into paychecks. He'd pour out a little liquor for them when he returned to the States—not much, because Trump Whiskey was expensive. But enough to say he'd done it, and that was all that mattered.

★ ★ ★ ★

Excerpt From the Trump/Dorset Sessions

May 23, 2018, 6:58 PM

PRESIDENT TRUMP: You're very lucky to be talking to me. I'm very busy now, you know. I have hundreds of very important meetings every week. You can't imagine how important these meetings are.

High-pressure negotiations, which I am very good at. I'm amazing at negotiating. I'm going to bring you to some meetings so you can see. You're going to love these meetings. I have the best meetings. Are you going to ask me any questions?

LESTER DORSET: Ah, yes . . . During your administration, the lawmaking process seems to have come to a standstill. You've vetoed nearly ninety percent of the bills that have crossed your desk.

TRUMP: You always reject the first offer.

DORSET: Both the House and Senate are controlled by Republicans. You would think they would be on common ground with you.

TRUMP: Listen, I may have campaigned as a Republican, but I'm no more a Republican than that crazy-haired garden gnome Bernie was a Democrat. That stuff's just letters after your name on the ballot; it doesn't mean anything. The GOP totally disrespected me.

DORSET: And now you're disrespecting them?

TRUMP: I don't forget. I don't forget, okay? So, yeah, there's a little bit of that. Bottom line, though, is that they're grandstanding. They're playing politics. I'm issuing executive orders.

DORSET: One of your signature projects, the Even Greater Wall, is only halfway complete because Congress refuses to fund your executive orders. Your critics have characterized it as the "Wall to Nowhere."

TRUMP: It has nothing to do with Congress. As you know, Mexico agreed to pay for the damned thing—just like I said they would. Unfortunately, their check bounced. Not a great way to convince the world your country's not full of rapists. Just saying. So construction has been halted for the time being. There's that saying, "Trump Tower wasn't built in a day." Nobody's ever undertaken a project of this magnitude before. Except for maybe the Chinese, who had a much smaller border to defend.

DORSET: The Great Wall of China is four thousand miles long; the US-Mexico border is just about half that.

TRUMP: US-Mexico is just the first phase. Phase two is the Canadian border. Five thousand more miles, baby. And let's not forget our borders with the oceans. Once Congress opens the purse for me, China can suck it.

DORSET: I wasn't aware there were any troubles with Canadians entering our country illegally. Or ... fish.

TRUMP: Securing our borders is about more than immigration. What if some Kardashian sneaks across with a dirty bomb? Somebody had to do something about the Kardashian problem. Nobody wanted to talk about it but me. So that's why you've seen me take other steps, like revoking Kim and Kanye's passports.

DORSET: This supposed connection between Kardashians and terrorism has been refuted many times over. The facts—

TRUMP: The fact is, there are terrorists everywhere over there—Iran, Kazakhstan, *and* Kardashia. You can't refute that.

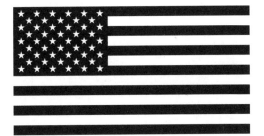

Monday, August 27, 2018

CHAPTER FIVE

★ ★ ★ ★

HAMMER TIME

Jimmie searched for glimpses of the new golden exterior of the White House through the buildings as his car drove up Connecticut Avenue. "Traffic on Sixteenth is restricted due to the glare issue," his driver said.

They inched through traffic, and—there it was. The gleaming columns, the burnished eaves. The word "TRUMP" spanning the facade.

It was all too beautiful to be real. People actually lived here? *Not people*, he thought. *The Trumps.*

The first family, like others before them, had moved into the White House's Executive Residence, which was sandwiched between the East and West Wings. From what Jimmie had read, there had been some chatter about building an entirely new residence on the grounds. A Trump Wing, financed entirely by Trump himself. However, Trump had ultimately decided against a new structure. The return on his investment would be nil—he couldn't take it with him when he left office. Donating it to the federal government was a ridiculous proposition even for the most altruistic philanthropist. Instead, the real estate mogul had overhauled the existing residence. Trump had even gone so far as to move the bedrooms to the third floor so that he could turn the second floor into one giant State Dining Room.

"We'll do a lap before we pull in," his driver said. The car circled the grounds, giving Jimmie a firsthand look at the new features he'd only seen on TV.

Turning down Constitution Avenue gave Jimmie a great view of the fountain. The Haupt Fountains may have been nice, but they were nothing compared to the Bellagio Fountains that Trump had shipped in from Vegas.

Through the cascades of water, Jimmie could see the new White House golf course on the South Lawn. Eisenhower had a putting green; Trump had an entire eighteen-hole course designed by Jack Nicklaus. From what he could see, the ninth green had almost recovered from its trampling during the 2018 Easter Egg Roll. President Trump had asked all the children to wear golf spikes, but it turned out most kids didn't have them. A week later, Trump launched his public-private initiative to provide golf shoes to underprivileged youth. It would have gone over better had he not slashed funding for science education a month earlier.

The car finally let Jimmie out near the surprisingly unassuming staff entrance. As he waited in the line to pass through the metal detectors, Jimmie looked over the large sign showing items he was forbidden to bring inside with him. The list now included hair dryers, after an event last month in which Trump had to be evacuated from a rally after a blow-dryer-armed protestor had gotten close enough to give Trump's hair a nearly fatal tousling.

"Any liquids, perishables, electronics, flammable material?" asked the guard as he unzipped Jimmie's backpack.

"No, sir," Jimmie replied. "Except—well, notebooks, which could be flammable. They're paper."

"What's this?" asked the guard, pulling Jimmie's micro-cassette recorder out of the bag.

"That's just my tape recorder," Jimmy said. "I'm going to be interviewing the president."

The guard nodded in understanding, placed the tape recorder on the table, and then smashed it to pieces with a hammer.

"Whoa! Hey! Come on, man! No!" Jimmy wailed. "Why did you do that? That recorder survived the Playboy Mansion!"

"No outside recording devices," the security guard said, trying on Jimmie's backpack. "This is nice. Is it new?"

Jimmie nodded. "Could I have it back now?"

"No backpacks allowed, sorry," the guard said. "You can buy it back later on eBay, unless you're outbid."

As much as Jimmie wanted to grumble about it, he knew that the heightened security measures were warranted. Even though most dissenters were fleeing the country, the occasional protestor still slipped through the iron gates with a can of white spray paint to "take back the White House."

Dissidents didn't have a leg to stand on, though. Trump had won the election in a landslide. Some commentators believed the "landslide" was more than just a metaphoric natural disaster. Jimmie had heard the 2016 election called the biggest single natural disaster in world history. Donald J. Trump, they said, was a meteor that was going to wipe the human race off the face of the earth. Trump had been in office for more than eighteen months now, and the human race was still going strong.

Trump was either the savviest or the luckiest president in history. His day-one repeal of Obamacare left millions of unemployed Americans uninsured. Without health care, they were dying in record numbers. The resulting drop in the unemployment rate sent the Dow skyrocketing.

To give him credit, he'd created jobs as well. Construction of the Keystone XXL Pipeline employed thousands. The Keystone XXL Oil Spill cleanup employed thousands more.

Trump had found creative ways to fund federal programs while lowering taxes. Who else would have thought to pay for FEMA's budget by suing the Catholic Church over property damage caused by acts of God?

And for every environmentalist who was furious about Secretary of the Energies Sarah Palin's "frack 'em all" policies, there were three consumers thrilled with the money they were saving at the pumps and on their heating bills.

Whether Trump had actually made America great again was a moot point—he made America *feel* great again. And if that meant that Jimmie would need to bid on his own backpack to get it returned to him? That was simply the price of greatness.

CHAPTER SIX

★ ★ ★ ★

THE APPRENTICE

A White House aide appeared as Jimmie was putting his change back into his pockets. "Mr. Bernwood? This way, please." He led Jimmie down a dimly lit, wood-floored hallway.

"Wow, the inside of this place is a lot less fancy than the outside," said Jimmie.

"The president believes in containing costs," explained the aide. "He had all the marble and brass removed from the staff areas and placed out where visitors and the public can see it. He said, 'Marble has wow factor, so why waste it on a bunch of secretaries and cooks?'"

"I guess I see his point," said Jimmie.

"Well, then, I think it's sad that you don't believe you deserve wow factor," said the aide. "Here's Miss Blythe's office."

He entered to find Emma smiling at him with her huge Miss Universe–quality anime eyes. Wow factor indeed.

"You look like an entirely new man, James."

He took the seat across the desk from her—gently, as he still had lower back pain from being shivved. The scar, however, looked totally rad in the mirror. Like a pink lightning bolt. Women were going to be super-impressed by it. Now Harry just needed to find his Hermione.

"You didn't like the beard?" he said, running a hand across his freshly shaved chin.

"When I visited you in the hospital, there was a scorpion in it."

All Jimmie could say was, "Alive or dead?"

Emma tossed him an employee manual. As she rifled through her filing cabinet, Jimmie marveled at how she looked even hotter than she had when he'd last seen her. Rare was the woman (or man) who looked better without a little medicated haze to smooth out the imperfections. Then again, Emma Blythe was a rare specimen.

As he'd learned via Wikipedia, she was a former Miss Universe winner from the United Kingdom who was now the White House apprentice. The position had formerly been known as chief of staff—a sort of personal assistant to the president. Though beauty pageant contestants got a bad rap from some in the femisphere, they were often intellectually heads and tails above their peers. Emma Blythe, for instance, had graduated at the top of her class from Cambridge. She was now the youngest chief of staff in history. If pageant contestants also had heads and tails above their peers, well, you couldn't very well hold that against them, could you? That would be discrimination. At least in Jimmie's book.

"Did they give you any trouble in security?" Emma asked.

"They took my tape recorder apart. With a hammer."

"I should have warned you about that. We'll provide you with one to use on-site—one that doesn't leave the White House under any conditions. One with an internal hard drive, to prevent tapes being lost. Until we get you on President Trump's schedule, however, you'll be free to use a notebook to record your informal observations."

"When will I get on his schedule? What sort of time frame are we looking at here?"

Emma leaned back in her chair and crossed her arms. "We're going to take this one day at a time. You're to be a fly on the wall. Like a child during the Victorian era. You're to be seen but not heard. Blend in with the background. The less anyone around here sees you, the better. Case in point: That jacket has to go."

The bright-blue suit jacket and American flag necktie had cost him nearly thirty bucks at JCPenney. Along with the generic white button-up shirt, they were the only "dress-up" clothes he owned. In fact, they were some of the only clothes he owned. He'd been living out of a duffle bag for a while now.

"If I could get an advance on my first paycheck—"

She opened her drawer and peeled five fifties off a stack of bills like she was a bank teller. "It's important to the president to always have cash on hand. Just remember to replace this after you get paid."

This was a pleasant surprise. He decided to push it. "Do we have a per diem for food? Because all I had for breakfast today was reheated Chipotle. Didn't have enough cash on me for the salmonella-free upgrade last night, so I spent half the night with my head in the toilet."

"If you got sick off something, why did you even keep the leftovers?"

He shrugged. As if on cue, his stomach rumbled.

"You can request reimbursement online," Emma said. "The cap is seventy-five dollars a day, though."

"I can . . . probably work with that."

So far, Jimmie was liking his new employer. He'd never been much for politics before, but he could get used to the expense-account lifestyle. Pity the clueless taxpayers who were going to be footing his bill.

"So where's he at?" Jimmie said. "The president."

"Most days, he'll be right on the other side of that door with the brass *T* on it, in the Oval Office. Right now, however, he's in a meeting with his top-level advisors. Once we have your dot-gov e-mail set up, you'll be receiving daily updates with President Trump's schedule. I don't think I have to tell you how important it is to keep this information to yourself. If somebody—some outside agitator—were to get ahold of such vital information . . ."

"Understood," he said. "My lips are sealed."

"You built an entire career out of digging up dirt on celebrities. I strongly doubt it was a one-way street. There's a fair amount of trading gossip in your line of work, am I right?"

He didn't say anything.

"I'm not judging you," she said. "It's not my call, anyway—it's the president's. And you're his guy. We had to give up considerable assets to bring you home. The relationship between our countries is strained at the moment, as you're well aware. President Trump sent me to personally negotiate the transaction."

"What'd they want for me?"

"Adam Sandler."

Jimmie nodded. Depending on your comedic sensibilities, America had either gotten the better of Mexico or been ripped off. "You said the president is a fan of mine. What about you? Have you read my stuff?"

"What I think is irrelevant."

"Just out of curiosity, what do you think?"

She leaned forward. He could see that her blue eyes were shaded with green. "What do I think? I think—"

The door behind Jimmie flew open, startling him. He turned to see a man clad in a sharp gray suit whose pits were sopping wet.

"We have a situation," the man said. "And it rhymes with 'muclear.'"

CHAPTER SEVEN

★ ★ ★ ★

FIRST IMPRESSIONS
ARE EVERYTHING

Jimmie's pulse shot through the gold-trimmed ceiling, but Emma was nonplussed. Maybe there was another word that rhymed with "muclear" besides the obvious. "Heather Locklear" almost rhymed. So did "Spooktacular." Had Heather Locklear pulled out of this year's White House Spooktacular?

"You couldn't have just phoned me?" Emma said. "I'm in the middle of something."

"Your phone went straight to voice mail," the man said. "The Security Council is convening in the Boardroom right now."

She found her phone in her desk drawer. "Could somebody dig up Steve Jobs's corpse and get it to make a phone that doesn't need to be charged every six hours?"

"We can find out who's in charge of Apple now and put some pressure on them," the man said. "Or, better yet, we can draft a bill mandating batteries on smartphones last seventy-two hours. And if they don't do it, we punch them in the face." He pulled out his own iPhone. "Hey, Siri, tell the CEO of Apple to call the White House pronto."

The phone beeped, and Siri's voice replied, "I've added it to his schedule for tomorrow at three PM eastern time."

The man caught Jimmie's astonished expression. "Come on," the guy said. "The amount of data these things collect on you—of course that works."

Emma tossed her phone back into the drawer. "Corey, I'd like you to meet Jimmie Bernwood. You'll be seeing him around quite a bit—he's President Trump's new ghostwriter. Jimmie, this is Corey Lewandowski, the press secretary. You may remember him as President Trump's campaign manager. Or maybe not."

Lewandowski crushed Jimmie's hand. "You've got some pretty big shoes to fill," the man said. Then he turned to Emma: "We've really got to hustle. They're waiting—"

"Fine, fine," she said, following Lewandowski out the door in a huff.

Jimmie watched them leave. He flexed the fingers of his right hand, trying to regain feeling. What was he supposed to do now? He didn't have a desk of his own, as far as he knew. She'd talked about setting him up with an e-mail, so he assumed he should find someone in their IT department. Even though he was sitting just a few steps away from the president of the United States' office, he was struck with déjà vu. It was that *Not only do I have no idea what's going on here, but I'm also not entirely sure anybody else knows, either* feeling.

Emma poked her head back into the office. "Well, are you coming?"

"He said something about a Security Council?" Jimmie asked. He swallowed a burp. "That sounds top secret. I didn't think I'd have clearance."

"That badge on your lanyard gives you the same clearance as the POTUS."

He fingered the badge. His clearance level was listed as "ORANGE." Just underneath a terrible picture of his face. Or maybe it wasn't the picture that was terrible—maybe it was his face. Shaving the beard had done him wonders, but there was that Sarah Palin saying: *You can't put lipstick on a pig.* Jimmie had grown up in rural Iowa, and damned if he didn't know that to be the truth.

"What's POTUS?" he asked, trailing Emma into the hallway.

"You really don't follow politics, do you? POTUS," she explained, "stands for President of Trump's United States."

Jimmie had the same security clearance as the president. The president of the United States. He couldn't believe it. Somebody had to have screwed up.

While they were waiting at the mirrored doors of the elevator, who to his wandering eyes should appear but Cat Diaz. She was on the warpath, absorbed in her phone, when she glanced at Jimmie out of the corner of her eye. She returned to her screen but immediately did a double take and slammed on the brakes.

"Jimmie," she said. There was a look of confusion on her face.

"Cat," he said. "You work here now? That's crazy, meeting like this."

Her gaze went straight down to his badge. As she read his clearance level, her brow only furrowed further.

My eyes are up here, he almost said but thought better of it. He was staring into her cleavage like it was the abyss.

"I'd heard you dropped off the grid," Cat said, looking up at him.

"Turns out, if you want to buy a clean pair of boxers, you need to get back on the grid."

The elevator opened behind him. "You can catch up later," Emma said, shoving him in so hard he almost knocked over the bonsai tree on the decorated pillar in the corner.

Jimmie gave a little wave to Cat as the doors slid shut. He had no idea why he'd brought up his boxers, but all in all, not a bad chance encounter. He was looking forward to catching up later—not romantically, of course. He kind of had an eye on Emma. Was there a Mr. Universe in the picture?

Emma pressed the button marked "B."

"The White House has a basement?" Jimmie asked.

"Why wouldn't it?"

"I don't know, I thought it was like the Alamo."

"The Alamo has a basement," she said. "It's a secret military facility. If you ever visit, take your badge along, and they'll be happy to give you the full tour."

"Next thing you know, you'll be telling me there are aliens at Area 51."

The elevator lurched. Jimmie's stomach fluttered.

"There aren't any aliens at Area 51," Emma said, staring ahead as they descended. "We keep them at Area 61."

"What's at Area 51, then?"

"Souvenir shops, mostly," she replied, "and the frozen big-foot corpse. But in 2021, the biggest Trump casino yet."

Before he could ask if she was kidding, the elevator came to an abrupt stop. Jimmie's stomach capsized. Its contents catapulted up his esophagus with violent speed. The doors slid open, and Jimmie Bernwood showered the president of the United States of America with half-digested rice and beans.

President Trump looked down at the former burrito dripping off his shirt and then glared at Jimmie. His lips were pursed in deliberation. After what seemed like an eternity, he spoke.

"I love Hispanics, but this is freaking ridiculous."

CHAPTER EIGHT

$$\star \ \star \ \star$$

THE GOOD, THE BAD, AND THE UGLY

The president stood tall and proud, as if expecting the vomit to apologize and leave on its own. Donald J. Trump wasn't one to faze easily. Most presidents' hair turned gray after eighteen months in office. If Trump's hair had changed at all, Jimmie would have to say it hadn't grayed but bronzed.

Dueling scents reached Jimmie's nose. The smell of his own stomach acid was being forced into submission by the president's cologne, which was unmistakably Success by Trump.

Jimmie took a rapid assessment of the situation to determine if things were really as bad as they seemed.

The good news was that President Trump could shower, change, and be back at work with only a minimal interruption to his day. That was one of the benefits of working in one's own home.

The bad news, at least for Jimmie, was that his status as a fly on the wall had been blown. Big time.

During the primary campaign, a female reporter had gotten a little too aggressive with her questioning of Trump and was manhandled by Lewandowski. There was video of the incident online, which showed the reporter wielding a pen—a "potentially dangerous weapon," according to Trump. As if a reporter could ever be a threat to somebody's welfare using just a pen. Years of sitting hunched over computer keyboards meant that it was usually a pain just to bend over and look into a fridge, let alone have the range of motion and athletic dexterity necessary to ram a ballpoint pen into somebody's throat.

If a reporter simply asking questions of a presidential candidate could be manhandled for being a threat, what was about to happen to a reporter who threw up on the president?

Jimmie Bernwood was about to find out.

Trump, who stood six foot three, towered over Jimmie as if he were twice that. The white circles under Trump's glaring eyes made Jimmie feel like he was pinned in a prison searchlight. Jimmie's shame was only seconds old, and already its weight was unbearable. He thought he'd reached the bottom of his shame spiral in Mexico, but clearly he was still circling the drain.

The elevator door began to close between them, but Trump stuck out his hand to stop it. As the door slid back open, Trump turned to the stoic Secret Service agent flanking him on the left. The agent's cleanly shaven dome glistened under the brilliant chandeliers. His eyebrows had been plucked to nonexistence. Jimmie wondered what he had against hair. Then he remembered who the guy had to guard all day. It made sense he might have developed some weird, obsessive behaviors regarding the maintenance of one's hair.

Trump barked at the agent, "Are you going to just stand there, or are you going to shoot this loser?"

CHAPTER 9

★ ★ ★ ★

YOU'RE FIRED

Sweat beaded on Jimmie's forehead and behind his ears. He hadn't even been aware that he had sweat glands back there.

The Secret Service agent made no motion to pull a gun out, however. He simply stood there, hands clasped together. "Where would you like me to shoot him, sir? I could aim for the torso—put a bullet right through his stomach and then wait for him to bleed to death on the floor of the elevator."

"Don't be an idiot," Trump said. "People need to use the elevator. Do it in the hallway."

"On this carpet?" the Secret Service agent said.

Trump looked down at his feet, and so did Jimmie. The bright-red carpet had a golden pattern woven into it. It looked brand new, like it had just been laid down this morning.

Emma stepped out of the elevator. Jimmie had been so caught up in his own drama, he'd forgotten she was still standing behind him.

She loosened the president's tie. Trump watched her work, a frown still plastered on his face.

"The first lady would not be happy if you ruined this carpet," Emma said. "Can you afford a fifth divorce?"

"Fourth divorce," Trump said. "My fourth marriage was annulled, remember?"

Emma used the tie to wipe off Trump's suit. "Regardless, you don't want to shoot your new ghostwriter. He wasn't an easy get. And after what happened with the last one . . ."

Trump now eyed Jimmie through the elevator door, which was closing again. Trump held out his hand, and Jimmie cautiously shook it.

"I wasn't shaking your hand," Trump said as the elevator door slid back open. "I don't need to catch whatever third-world Zima virus you picked up down in Mexico. I have a country to run."

The hallway beyond them was empty, unlike the rest of the White House, which was buzzing with activity. There was a single set of double doors at the end of the corridor. The Boardroom.

"Would you still like me to kill him, sir?" the Secret Service agent asked.

"That won't be necessary," Trump said. "Just shoot him in the kneecaps."

The Secret Service agent reached a hand inside his jacket. Before he could pull his handgun out, Trump held up a hand to call him off.

"I'm kidding," Trump said. "Jesus Christ, you guys take everything so seriously."

The agent produced a pack of Mentos from his jacket. "I wasn't reaching for my gun. We're not authorized to shoot anybody unless they're a direct threat to your well-being. And this guy . . . well, look at him."

"You'd take a bullet for me," Trump said.

"Without a second thought."

"You'd jump on a live grenade."

"Of course, sir."

"But you won't shoot somebody when I tell you to?" Trump turned to Emma. "Can I fire this guy? Can I fire the entire Secret Service and replace them with my own security detail? Is that a thing I can do?"

"We've been over this before," she said. "Not only are they authorized to protect you, but they are also compelled to by law. According to Title 18, Section 3056, neither you nor the vice president may decline their protection."

Trump snorted. He turned to Jimmie, who still hadn't spoken a word in the presence of his new boss. "Not only is she beautiful, but she's brilliant as shit," Trump said. "You ever watch the Miss Universe pageant?"

"Can't say that I have," Jimmie said.

It was, perhaps, not the right thing to say after what he'd just done. But Trump just laughed and shook his head. "Nobody watches TV anymore, do they? For the longest time, I kept that dying medium alive with *The Apprentice*. But nowadays, it's all about steaming this, steaming that."

"Streaming," Emma said, gently correcting him.

"You know what I mean," Trump said.

Emma turned to the Secret Service agent. "Page Chris Christie and have him send someone to clean this mess up." She handed him Trump's tie. "And do something with this."

"So is that how it's going to be?" the agent said, angrily snatching the tie from her. "This job keeps getting better and better. You know, we're not even supposed to hold the president's coat. We're not supposed to—"

Trump cut him off. "Be careful, or I will find a way to fire you—all of you men in black. By God, I will find a way." Trump paused. "And grow some fucking eyebrows."

"Well," Emma said, "if you will excuse us, Mr. President, we need to get to the Boardroom."

Trump snorted. "I was just on the way there myself but had to head back up to the Oval Office to pick up my comb. Let the Security Council know I'll be a few minutes late, would you?"

"It was a pleasure meeting you, Mr. President," Jimmie said as Emma whisked him away.

"Wish I could say the same about you," Trump called out after them.

When they were well out of earshot, Emma tore into Jimmie.

"What the bloody hell was that all about? You made me look like a bloody fool. Why didn't you apologize?" she hissed. "What the hell is wrong with you?"

"I heard he didn't like it when people apologize," Jimmie said. "That he sees it as a sign of weakness. He's never apologized in his life."

Emma paused in front of the double doors. "If, in the future, you throw up on somebody—especially if it's the president of the United States of America—you apologize."

She swiped her badge and waited for the light to go green. While he had never paid much attention to politics, he'd done some reading online to prepare for his first day on the job. The former Situation Room was the brainchild of John F. Kennedy. Although Trump had rechristened it the "Boardroom," this was the same room where Bush had given the orders to invade Iraq. Where Obama had orchestrated SEAL Team Six's assassination of bin Laden. Where Bill Clinton had probably gotten a handy or two.

Emma held the door open, and Jimmie stepped into the darkened room. Somehow, they'd beat Lewandowski down here. Jimmie ran his hand along the wall to the right. "Is there a light switch in—"

"SURPRISE!!!"

CHAPTER TEN

★ ★ ★ ★

SURPRISE! YOU'RE DEAD!

At the sound of the party horns, Jimmie jumped a half foot into the air. If his shoes hadn't been Velcroed on tight enough, he might have leapt right out of them.

Emma caught him as he fell backward and helped him stay upright. He stared with confusion at the assembled group of revelers who had thrown him for a loop. The looks of shock on their faces were in stark contrast to the pointed party hats on their heads.

"Who in Trump's name is this bozo?" an old white guy asked. Jimmie was in the middle of a sea of old white guys. He blinked, trying to process what he was seeing. Eventually, the old white guys resolved into individual faces. There was Lewandowski, who'd already arrived after all. Secretary of Transportation Eastwood. Secretary of Defense Nugent. The newest members of the Supreme Court, Justices Giuliani and Philbin. The only person who didn't fit the profile was Donald Trump Jr., a slightly younger white guy.

"This," said Emma, "is Trump's new ghostwriter, Jimmie Bernwood."

"Did we ever find out what happened to the last guy?" some suit-and-tie said. "He went off backpacking the Pacific Crest Trail after reading *Wild*, and then . . ."

A sea of disapproving faces turned on the schmuck who'd asked the question. Jimmie was too panicked to really care about "the last guy" right now.

Emma guided Jimmie to a leather chair at the head of the long table, which filled the center of the room. He started breathing again. Oxygen was good. Oxygen was very, very good. He loved oxygen like A-list actors loved nannies.

"And here he is! President Donald Trump!" shouted Justice Philbin as Trump entered the room. Everyone again yelled, "SURPRISE!!!"

Jimmie was ready for it this time. He barely broke a sweat. How Trump had changed so fast, he had no idea. Perhaps he had a pit crew of stylists standing by at all times, ready to change him like a race car with a blown tire.

The room burst into song.

"FOR HE'S A JOLLY GOOD FELLOW, FOR HE'S A JOLLY GOOD FELLOW . . ."

Jimmie mouthed along. He was slightly distracted by the world map plastered on the giant video screen covering the far wall. There were a number of red dots inching their way across the Atlantic Ocean. To an untrained observer like Jimmie, it appeared that American battleships were converging just off British shores. It was a little disturbing, to say the least. He tuned back in to the song just in time for the second verse.

"HE FINALLY OVERTURNED NAFTA, HE FINALLY OVERTURNED NAFTA, HE FINALLY OVERTURNED NAFTA, WHICH NOBODY CAN DENY!"

"Thank you, everyone, thank you! We did it!" shouted Trump over the hubbub. "Global warming—now *that's* something we can all deny!"

The crowd roared with laughter. The Nuge set a large cake on the table. It had an image of Calvin from *Calvin and Hobbes* urinating on a crude drawing of the US Capitol Building. It was like one of those decals Jimmie had seen along the border, which had the cartoon character pissing onto the word "Mexico."

As the crowd moved in on the cake and Giuliani's shrill cries of "I want a corner! I want a corner!" grew louder, Jimmie's attention drifted back to the video screen. Something was happening off the coast of the United Kingdom, all right. But as the graphic repeated itself over and over, Jimmie dismissed it as nothing he needed to be concerned with. Although relations between the United States and the United Kingdom had cooled off considerably since Trump took office, this was the former Situation Room. Trump and his Security Council ran through different situations at this table. Just because a graphic had been put together didn't mean it was happening—or was even going to happen. It was just a situation. One of hundreds, perhaps.

Trump smacked John McCain on the back. "Hey there, Johnny boy! They let you out! Wait—can I say that?"

"Actually, Mr. President, I was hoping to ask you a quick question. It's about a spending issue with—"

"What is it with you guys? Always politics," Trump interrupted. "Come in for a meeting next week. I never talk business when there's cake—rule fourteen in *The Art of the Deal: The Expanded Coloring Book Edition.* You gotta lighten up a little, Johnny."

"Well, at least I tried," said McCain with a good-natured laugh before sulking toward the exit. Trump didn't notice; he'd already moved on to the owner of the Washington Wizards, Ted Leonsis.

"Ted. Teddy. Hope the NBA doesn't mind—it's going to take a little longer to expand into Mexico. Necessary evil. This is such a great, great move otherwise for our country. More jobs means more butts in the seats at your games, though, am I right?"

Jimmie kicked himself for leaving his notebook in Emma's office. Some biographer he was. He was trying to jot down notes in frosting on the back of his hand but was concerned it would melt away before he could transcribe it. He would have to be better prepared tomorrow.

If he still had a job tomorrow. What was it that guy had said? *Did we ever find out what happened to the last guy?* Even if he wasn't fired for throwing up on the president, Jimmie worried that he wouldn't be holding onto this job for very long.

CHAPTER ELEVEN

★ ★ ★ ★

THE WHOLE SHACK SHIMMIES

Somebody cranked up The B-52s' "Love Shack" on the surround sound stereo system. The map on the video screen dissolved into an iTunes screen saver. For a meeting room, the Boardroom had some serious bass. Probably needed it for all the videos of explosions.

To Jimmie's dismay, the cake was chocolate. Not really Jimmie's thing. He was more of a vanilla guy, at least as far as desserts went. He'd accepted a piece, however. He didn't want to be "that guy"—you know, the prissy coworker whose tastes are so specific that you'd probably catch them wanking at work before you caught them eating carbs.

Oh, who was he kidding? He already *was* "that guy"— the one who'd thrown up on the president on his first day on the job. If word hadn't spread yet, it would soon. Not that he'd ever been one to mingle with his coworkers.

You're a journalist, he told himself, trying to swallow the sponge cake without making a face. *These aren't your coworkers— these are your subjects.* And then another thought crossed his mind: *You're not a journalist. Not any longer. Not when one of your subjects is bankrolling you.*

A big-bottomed guido took the empty chair next to Jimmie. Chris Christie. Although the job title on his badge said he was the "chief janitor," Christie wasn't dressed like a janitor. His navy-blue suit and power-red tie were the same as every else's in the Boardroom, albeit from the "big-and-tall" section. The *really* big-and-tall section.

"You look like you're having fun," Christie said, leering at Jimmie.

"Just some first-day jitters. And maybe a little food poisoning."

"Been there before," Christie said, shoving a fork right into what was left of the cake. "First day in the governor's office, I was so nervous that I shit my drawers. It was a little bit of excitement, a little bit of Montezuma's revenge."

"No shit."

"*Yes* shit," Christie said.

Jimmie watched as Christie shoveled the cake into his gullet like a bank robber stuffing bundles of cash into a duffle bag.

"So what did you do?" Jimmie asked. "After you . . . shit your drawers."

Christie wiped the yellow frosting from around his mouth. "I ordered up a traffic study in Fort Lee, put the kybosh on a new tunnel to Manhattan, and then cleaned myself up in the bathroom of Jerry Jones's G5 en route to the Super Bowl. The bathroom in that plane is nicer than anything on the ground in Trenton."

"So the moral of the story is . . ."

"There is no moral to the story," Christie said. "Morals are for putzes. You understand what I'm saying, Jimmie?"

"I think so," Jimmie said. He really had no idea what the hell Christie's point was, other than the fact that you couldn't count on anyone who worked for you to tell you when your shit stank. "Say . . . do you know anything about this 'nuclear' situation? The press secretary mentioned there was an emergency that rhymed with 'muclear.'"

Christie snorted. "That's just the Security Council code we use when there's dessert in the Boardroom."

"So what's the code when there's a real nuclear emergency?"

"Same thing."

Jimmie felt his eyes go wide. "Isn't that . . . dangerous?"

Christie narrowed his eyes to the point where his pupils were crushed into two tiny, black coals. "I see those hamsters running on those wheels in your head," he said. "You're not an idiot. Not like half the reporters upstairs in the White House press corps. The president wanted you for this job, though—Lord knows why, but he did. I know you're dangerous. A wise guy like you, around here? You could hurt people, real easily, with that pen of yours. I'm talking about your words, of course. You writers and your weak stabbing motions. Just remember: You could also *get* hurt . . . real easily. And we wouldn't want that. Trust me—I do a lot of 'cleaning up' for President Trump, if you know what I mean. Ask yourself, are you the froster? Or the frosting?"

Christie crammed the last of the cake into his gaping maw. "See you around, kid," he mumbled.

Jimmie sat in stunned silence. If he didn't know any better, he'd have thought the former governor of New Jersey had just threatened him. In his line of work, he'd been used to being threatened—by lawyers, usually. Never by a janitor.

Jimmie was beginning to sense that something . . . untoward might have happened to this mysterious predecessor. The ghostwriter who had left behind "big shoes to fill," according to the press secretary. Big . . . concrete shoes?

CHAPTER TWELVE

★ ★ ★ ★

A HARD BED IS GOOD TO FIND

Jimmie Bernwood returned to the Royal Linoleum Hotel—
"VACUUMED DAILY," according to the neon sign—well
after dark. He'd gone suit shopping, which meant forgoing the
chauffeured car he'd arrived at work in for public transportation.
He'd spent an extra forty-five minutes waiting on the Metro,
which had stopped running during yet another electrical black-
out. So far, he'd learned that when the trains did run on time, you
could be sure the buses wouldn't. And good luck hailing a taxi—
Uber had put most of them out of business, just before getting
put out of business themselves by Bikinibus. Washington's entire
traffic system was a mess . . . which, he supposed, was a good anal-
ogy for the government. Nothing prepared you better for working
in DC like living in DC. Even when things were rolling along
smoothly, you sensed there was a wreck just around the corner.

He fumbled with his keys. A prostitute passed by with a
john. Jimmie should have taken Emma's offer to put him up in
a Trump hotel last week. At least the hookers there would be
high-class—the kind that accepted Bitcoin instead of Starbucks
gift cards.

But it hadn't felt right to him. Even though he knew this was the lowest of the low in journalistic gigs—a celebrity ghost-writer who'd signed a nondisclosure agreement (a gag order, basically)—he needed some measure of independence. He was drawing the line at the daily allowance for food. The whole situation reminded him of when he'd dated Cat while working under her at the *Daily Blabber*. Time apart was a good thing. A healthy thing. Even if you didn't think you needed it, you needed it. Well, until one of you goes off and screws some guy from the *New York Times*.

He flopped down on the bed with the weight of a lead-filled corpse. It was like landing at the bottom of a rock quarry. The only thing harder than the criminals at the Royal Linoleum Hotel were the beds.

A deep moan issued forth from the other side of the wall.

He lifted his head. There was a low grunt, followed by another moan.

Yes. Yes. Harder.

There was a sharp knock on the wall between the rooms, and then another. Somebody was getting some use out of the beds, at least.

Jimmie grabbed a pillow and wrapped it around the back of his head, covering his ears. He needed to get to sleep soon. He had to be back at the White House in less than twelve hours, and if he didn't get a solid ten hours of shut-eye, he was a cranky bastard. Maybe when they finally assigned him an office, he could just sleep under the desk.

You like that? Say my name . . . say my name.

Teddy Mac.

Jimmie lifted the pillow and sat up. Teddy Mac? It couldn't be. It wasn't possible. No way. He pressed an ear up to the wall, which appeared to be nothing more than wallpaper over plywood.

Who's your daddy?

I don't know . . . oooooh . . . I've never met him . . . ahhhhh . . .

Son of a bitch.

Although the headboard continued to hit the wall, Jimmie knew with 100 percent certainty that the voices weren't coming from whoever was doing the bed-shaking. The voices were from the television, which was turned up to cover whatever action was really going on next door. Whoever was on the other side of the wall was watching the sex tape that had landed Jimmie Bernwood in hot water. Scalding-hot water. Boiling water that had ultimately cost him his job at the *Daily Blabber*.

They were watching the Ted Cruz sex tape.

CHAPTER THIRTEEN

★ ★ ★ ★

WALLBANGER

Jimmie phoned the front desk. The man with the Kardashian accent answered. It was the same man who'd given him the keys to the room. Actually, the only man who appeared to work at the Royal Linoleum Hotel besides the housekeepers. Jimmie explained that he wanted to file a noise complaint.

"I'm trying to get some sleep, and these guys—well, you can hear for yourself," Jimmie said, holding the phone receiver up to the wall. The pounding continued. "You hear that?"

"I can hear it from here," the man at the front desk said wearily.

"Well, aren't you going to do something about it?"

"It should be over soon. In my experience, these things never last more than eight or nine minutes. Especially with how vigorous they are going at it. By the time I got up from my desk and walked over there—well, they'd be vaping on the balcony."

Jimmie slammed the phone down. Eight or nine minutes? The sex tape went on for a full two and a half hours. It was as long and grueling as *Batman v Superman*. In fact, the tape was so grim and gritty at points that some believed it had also been directed by Zack Snyder.

It had been played so many times during the jury trial that it was burned into Jimmie's mind. Sometimes at night, when he closed his eyes, the candidate's smarmy visage slithered across his field of vision. In night-vision green, which impossibly made him look even creepier. To this day, Jimmie couldn't hear Pitbull's "Timber" without thinking of the rattling venetian blinds, Cruz's saggy pecs, and the squeaking.

Dear God, the squeaking.

It wasn't surprising somebody was watching it in the next room. The video had spread far and wide after he'd posted it in full on the *Daily Blabber*. Once a sex tape gets out, there's no putting that genie back into the bottle of lube. Everyone and their mother had seen it; some people had probably watched it with their mothers. Jimmie wasn't one to judge.

What bothered him, however, was that whoever was on the other side of the wall had started playing it just as he arrived home for the day. Was somebody taunting him?

There was something else nagging him, too. It took him a few more minutes to figure it out. When he did, it was as obvious as Jimmie's day had been long: The knocking of the headboard against the wall didn't have the regular ebb and flow of a couple making whoopee. It came and went in odd fits:

BUMP-BUMP-BUMP-BUMP-BUMP.

BUMP-BUMP.

BUMP-BUMP-BUMP-BUMP-BUMP.

It reminded him of the rhythmic code used by the human traffickers in California, the ones he'd been embedded with. They'd used it over the phone, though, and not through a wall. Was someone tapping out a message?

Listen to yourself, Jimmie, he thought. *Only in Washington for a week, and already you're seeing conspiracies. Get your head checked, or get out of town.*

51

That was one thought—that was what he wanted to think. But what he wanted to be true and what was true were probably two very different things. It wasn't a conspiracy theory if it checked out; it was just a conspiracy.

BUMP-BUMP-BUMP-BUMP.

BUMP.

BUMP-BUMP-BUMP-BUMP-BUMP—

Jimmie searched for a pen and paper. Inside the bedside drawer, he found a Royal Linoleum Hotel ballpoint pen. No paper—the closest he could find was a Gideon Bible.

He opened it to the title page and began recording the knocking on the wall as hash marks.

After he'd filled two pages of the Bible, a pattern emerged. He'd recorded the same message twice now. Whoever was over there was going to keep banging it out (pun intended), but he had enough to go on now.

It was definitely the same code used by the smugglers: Morris code. It had been invented by some woman named Katie Morris, who felt that Morse code was too complicated. (Jimmie happened to agree with her.) The idea was simple: The number of taps between each pause corresponded to a letter of the alphabet. One tap for *A*, two for *B*, and so on. He translated the message as:

MEETMEINCLINTONPLAZAATMIDNIGHT-
TELLNOONELEAVEYOURPHONEBEHINDY-
OURLIFEISINDANGER

Which could be parsed as:

MEET ME IN CLINTON PLAZA AT MIDNIGHT.
TELL NO ONE. LEAVE YOUR PHONE BEHIND.
YOUR LIFE IS IN DANGER.

Jimmie had plenty of questions. Meet *where* in Clinton Plaza? How would he recognize who he was supposed to be meeting? Why not pick a meeting place without a *Z* in its name? (Those twenty-six taps had taken *forever*.) For that matter, why not cut a few words out of that message? It was quarter past ten already. Had this guy never sent a code before? And if Jimmie's life were truly in danger, why not just tell him face-to-face right now? They were just some cheap wood and insulation apart. Why meet clandestinely in a park at the witching hour?

Jimmie rapped on the wall with knuckles to begin his own Morris code message. Before he got to his third rap, the television went silent. Jimmie heard the door open and close. There were footsteps on the stairs. His neighbor was on the run.

Jimmie rushed onto the outdoor balcony that connected the hotel rooms. He leaned over the second-floor railing. He couldn't see anybody down in the parking lot. Whoever had been next door was gone. But he knew where the mysterious wallbanger would be in just a few short hours. The same place he would be: Clinton Plaza.

CHAPTER FOURTEEN

★ ★ ★ ★

WE HONOR AND REMEMBER THEIR SACRIFICE

Jimmie strolled through the park, kicking a hypodermic needle along the sidewalk like a can. Though the pathway was well lit, Clinton Plaza was still a war zone of drug users, transients, and anonymous-sex seekers. And it was all by design.

One of Trump's earliest executive actions was to have the Federal Bureau of Land Management take over Logan Park. It had long been known as the most degenerate of public spaces in the city. Instead of cleaning it up, however, Trump simply renamed it after his Democratic rival. With the twelve-acre land under federal jurisdiction, local authorities stopped patrolling it at night. Trump conveniently didn't approve funds to staff it with federal officers, and things went downhill even further. On a scale of one to ten for safety, Clinton Plaza scored just under a Trump rally.

Clinton Plaza was only a short walk from where Jimmie was staying. He arrived about fifteen minutes ahead of time. At least, that was his estimate—he'd left his government-issued phone back at the hotel. Now that he was here, though, he kind of wished he had ignored the stranger's request to leave his phone behind. What if it was all a ruse to get him away from his room so that somebody could ransack it?

The phone was useless without his thumbprint. But there was always a chance they could lift his prints from the bottle of coconut oil beside the bed and cast a replica of his thumb, and—

Okay, now you're moving from "conspiracy theories" into "hospitalization" territory, he told himself. *All that's missing is for you to hear voices.*

As if on cue, he started hearing voices. Whispers from an element-battered tent; a hushed argument taking place somewhere deep in the woods. Closer to him, the chirping of a house finch. The same type of bird that had landed on Bernie's podium at a Portland rally. The poor bird had become an unofficial symbol of the last of the protestors in America.

Jimmie kicked the needle into the grass and picked up his pace. He was headed nowhere in particular, but he was in a hurry to get there. Whoever wanted to meet him would find him.

He stopped at the polished granite wall in the center of the park. The structure stood ten feet tall and stretched at least fifty feet along the pathway. There were hundreds of names engraved on it. The plaque bearing the wall's name and dedication was covered in moss. One word was visible: BENGHAZI.

So this was the Benghazi Memorial. Jimmie remembered the press conference where Trump had announced it. Speaking alongside his then wife Megyn Kelly, Trump had said, "Let us remember the sacrifices made in the wake of Hillary Clinton's terrible, embarrassing foreign policy disasters when she was the worst secretary of state in history."

"What a joke," a voice said from behind Jimmie.

Jimmie glanced over his shoulder. A solidly built man clad in a gray hoodie and jeans had crept up behind him. He didn't know if this was some random weirdo or the person who'd tapped out the code. Either way, Jimmie had to assume he was dangerous.

"A joke?" Jimmie said. "People died over there."

"Read the plaque."

"It's covered in moss."

"Then wipe it off," the man said with growing irritation.

"I've never liked moss," Jimmie said. "It feels weird. It's furry."

"Cats are furry, and people pet them all the time."

"They're not green. Most of them, at least."

The man crossed in front of Jimmie and, with his hand wrapped in his jacket, wiped the plaque off. He stepped back and let Jimmie read the bronze tablet bolted into the stone:

IN MEMORY OF THE MEN AND WOMEN
WHO SERVED ON THE HOUSE SELECT COMMITTEE ON BENGHAZI
AND SO VALIANTLY GAVE OF THEIR TIME
WE HONOR AND REMEMBER THEIR SACRIFICE

Jimmie took a closer look at the engravings that spanned the length of the wall. "Trey Gowdy, SC-04," he read aloud. "Susan Brooks, IN-05. Jim Jordan, OH-04. Mike Pompeo . . . KS-04." There were eight more names in the sequence before they repeated—a total of twelve names.

"This isn't the Benghazi Memorial," the stranger said. "It's the Benghazi *Hearings* Memorial. It's a memorial for the politicians who wasted their time interrogating Hillary Clinton about the Benghazi attacks. I'm no fan of hers, but the Right continues to treat her like she's some kind of war criminal. The man who built this could care less that four Americans died that night in Libya."

"And the man who built this wall . . ."

"Is your new boss," the stranger said. "Welcome to Washington, Mr. Bernwood."

CHAPTER FIFTEEN

★ ★ ★ ★

HOPE IS A
FOUR-LETTER WORD

"**I** hope you didn't invite me here to debate politics," Jimmie said, keeping a few paces between him and his new best friend. "Because I ain't that guy."

The man removed his hood. He wasn't a man so much as a boy—a baby-faced boy, at that. He had short, cropped blond hair, mostly hidden by a backward blue baseball cap. He was half a foot taller than Jimmie and at least ten years younger. It would have surprised Jimmie if the kid was old enough to buy a drink.

"No phone?" the kid said.

Jimmie shook his head.

"Good. Be careful with that thing—they're tracing your every step. Recording every conversation within range when it's powered on."

That didn't seem possible to Jimmie, but he kept that to himself. What did this kid know? Well, probably more about technology than he did, but still. Jimmie Bernwood had been around the block a few times, especially when it came to hidden recordings.

"Connor Brent," the kid said without offering a hand.

"And you know who I am, apparently," Jimmie said.

"You're the new ghostwriter."

He'd signed an NDA. Nobody was supposed to know about his involvement with the project outside of the White House. Not even the publisher, Crooked Lane.

"Oh, come on," Connor said. "Don't act dumb. The White House visitor logs are public. Everyone who walks through that front door—tourist or staff member, doesn't matter—is tracked online at WhiteHouse.gov. You signed in to see the apprentice. Reporters don't get that kind of access, especially not a blogger."

Blogger? Oh, hell no.

That prep-school accent made Jimmie eager to slap him across the face. The only reason he didn't do it was because he was afraid of cutting his palm on those sharp cheekbones.

Those sharp, perfect cheekbones.

"I'm a journalist," Jimmie said. "Use the B-word again, and I walk."

"Calm your tits, bro," Connor said. "I'm not here to start some fight over the state of modern journalism. In fact, we have mad respect for what you did to Cruz."

That whole fiasco had been a mistake. Good to know he had a few fanboys out there. However, politics had never been all that sexy to Jimmie. Ever since his mother lined his crib with the *National Enquirer*, he'd been fascinated with the world of celebrity. Politics, even when there was scandal involved, just didn't do it for him. This kid had him confused with somebody who gave two shits.

"You said my life was in danger," Jimmie said.

Connor's eyes danced furtively around the park. "The Donald's last ghostwriter ended up in the Rose Garden with a broken neck. Somebody threw him off the roof."

"That would have been all over the news."

"A tourist accidentally caught it on camera. They turned it into a GIF, and it went around the dark web. Not a single 'real' news site picked it up. Granted, the video was dark and blurry . . . but this was no Loch Ness Monster."

"Say what you're saying is true. What's that have to do with me?"

"The last guy in your position reached out to us. Apparently, he'd recorded some interviews with the president, and they yielded some game-changing information. His words, not ours. Unfortunately, he was dead before he could get the tapes out of the White House. Needless to say, whatever was on those tapes was big enough to kill somebody over."

"You have no idea what this information was?"

Connor shook his head.

"You keep saying 'we.' I assume you're, what, Democrats?"

"I'm a former Bernie bro."

"Former?" Jimmie said.

"No one's seen him since the Democratic National Convention," Connor said. "But we're carrying on his work. We don't believe in the two-party system. While most of us are former Bernie bros, anyone is welcome to join the Socialist Justice Warriors. Anyone who believes America should live up to the inscription at our door: 'Give me your tired, your poor, your huddled masses yearning to breathe free.' Trump doesn't even care that the masses are huddling.

"Help us," Connor continued. "Help us make America great again—again."

Make America great again . . . again?

"Sorry," Jimmie said, "I don't have any interest in joining your little after-school club. But your secret is safe with me—I don't have any interest in exposing it, either."

"That's good."

"Why? Because otherwise you'd have to kill me?"

Connor shook his head. "It's not us you have to worry about. And I think you already know that."

"I said it once, I'll say it again: You've got the wrong guy."

"Really?" Connor said. "You're a smart guy. Just look around you: The United States isn't a democracy anymore—it's a monarchy. We're walling ourselves off from the world, and the world can feel that. Support for the presidency may be at an all-time high within our country, but resentment of our country internationally is higher than it's been in decades. The resentment surpassed the W era a week into Trump's presidency. *A week.* He called Angela Merkel a 'dried-up six' *in his inaugural address.* The Donald is a dangerous man. He has dangerous friends. He's got his finger on the nuclear button, and he's involved in some sort of Twitter war with Prince Charles. What if the Twitter beef spills over into the real world?"

"So you think I can feed you some inside dirt, is that it? Something that will finally erode Trump's support at home and force him out of office. And then what?"

Connor said nothing.

"We're not going to war with the UK," Jimmie said. "But if we did, it wouldn't be the first time we've fought them. As

Trump has said on Twitter, 'We've kicked their ass before; we could do it again.' I hope it won't come to that, but you know how Trump is. He's mostly full of hot air."

"Say it's not just talk this time. The war won't just be between us and the UK," Connor said. "If a skirmish breaks out, Russia's jumping in. Then anyone else who wants to redivide the map in Europe. It's going to be World War III. The planet is going to go up in flames. That doesn't bother you?"

"The president needs congressional approval to go to war—even I know that," Jimmie said. "They haven't seen eye to eye on anything."

"He's wearing them down," Connor said. "Look, the guy had the country declare bankruptcy, and Congress impeached him. Then he sent the bulldozers in to seize all that private land along the border without authorization—do you remember that? And Congress impeached him. Then he lied under oath that he didn't write that list ranking the entire White House staff in order of 'bangability,' and Congress impeached him. Each time, not only was he exonerated, but his approval rating went up, and Congress's went down.

"Now, with the midterms coming up, they're feeling the pressure," Connor continued. "Trump's found even more leverage. He gets the roll calls of the votes on every bill and donates ten thousand dollars to the primary challenger of everyone who didn't vote his way. Then he calls the congressmen to tell them that he did it!"

"The American people know a bully when they see one," Jimmie said. "There will be an outcry eventually."

"Haven't you seen the polls? Americans don't like bullies in schoolyards, but they love it when the victim of the bullying is Congress. Change.org has forty thousand signatures on a petition for Trump to give Rand Paul a wedgie on the Senate floor. Trust me, bro. If Trump wants to go to war, we're going to war."

Jimmie shook his head. It sounded like this kid had been watching too much MSNBC. "I'm going to forget we had this conversation. I expect you to do the same," he said, turning to leave.

"Have you been to the basement?"

Jimmie froze. "Of the White House?"

"Of the Alamo," the kid said sarcastically. "Of course I mean the White House."

"Maybe. What of it?"

"There's another basement—a basement under the basement."

"A subbasement. That's not unusual."

"That's where his office was," Connor said. "It's a long shot, but his tapes might still be there. You might—"

"Whose tapes?"

"The last ghostwriter," Connor said. "Lester Dorset."

CHAPTER SIXTEEN

★ ★ ★ ★

WINTER IS COMING

Jimmie retraced his steps back toward the hotel. He'd known kids like Connor Brent back in college. Kids with Che Guevara T-shirts and hemp necklaces. Kids who camped out on the steps of the college president's office for "change."

That was all they ever wanted: "change." They knew what they were against but didn't have the imagination to think up a viable alternative. Jimmie wasn't much different. He didn't *like* war, but he wasn't foolish enough to think he could devise a better alternative to the way things were. True intelligence meant knowing the limits of your intelligence.

Jimmie had reached the limits of his intelligence long ago.

The kid was wrong—as kids often were.

There was no way Trump would ever give the order to fire nukes. If Jimmie knew the phrase "mutually assured destruction," Trump had to know it too. The man owned too much real estate to let it all go up in a mushroom cloud.

What bothered Jimmie a little, though, was this whole business with Lester Dorset.

He had specifically asked Emma Blythe if Cat and Lester were still together, and she'd artfully dodged the question. Even more suspicious, she hadn't said a word about the Pulitzer Prize–winning reporter being the previous ghostwriter.

There was a perfectly acceptable reason for her to avoid such talk: She might have sensed some professional animosity between Jimmie and Lester. That Jimmie felt inadequate next to somebody with the pedigree of a *New York Times* byline.

Well, the joke was on her. Jimmie couldn't care less about any of that. So what if he won a Pulitzer? It was for feature writing—the easy Pulitzer. Find a sob story, crap out ten thousand words, hello, Joe.

What he did care about, though, was the fact that Lester had—rather abruptly—overtaken Jimmie in Cat Diaz's affections. Did it bother Jimmie that his girlfriend had left him for that old bag of bones? Of course. But he'd let go of his anger long ago. Cat had made a choice—a dumb choice, but it was her business. He'd moved on.

Jimmie paused at the water fountain at the entrance to the park. The bronzed sculpture of Bill Clinton not having sexual relations with Monica Lewinsky glimmered under the moonlight. A soft breeze blew through the park, kicking up leaves. Jimmie shuddered as a chill came over him.

He tried to tell himself the chill was just because he didn't have on a heavy enough jacket. Fall was here, and the nights were getting longer and colder. The chill had nothing to do with the nagging suspicion that even if the kid was full of shit, some of what he'd said had resonated with Jimmie. That America, while strong at home, was assuming the reputation outside her borders of the crazy guy you cross the street to avoid. That the map he'd seen in the Boardroom was more than a simulation. That it wasn't just winter that was coming—it was war.

Excerpt From the Trump/Dorset Sessions

June 1, 2018, 9:45 AM

DORSET: Your relationship with Russian president Vladimir Putin has raised some eyebrows.

TRUMP: It's strictly platonic.

DORSET: Of course—I wasn't implying otherwise. You are, however, aware that Putin's record on human rights has earned him an F from Amnesty International. What do you think it says to the world when the American president is seen horseback riding with somebody like that?

TRUMP: You mean somebody who looks phenomenal without a shirt on? Somebody who's in tremendous, tremendous shape?

DORSET: I mean somebody who's been sanctioned by the United Nations multiple times. Somebody who was the target of a congressional resolution that condemned him as a threat to America's national security.

TRUMP: Is he a little rough around the edges? Yeah. It takes big balls to hold onto power in a place like Russia. They're a tough people. Very tough to govern.

But he's got *cojones* the size of grapefruits. Trust me—I know. I've been in the locker room with him.

DORSET: What did you think about Russia harboring NSA whistleblower Edward Snowden?

TRUMP: If I were in Putin's boots, I would have rolled out the red carpet for him too. What a smart thing to do. Russia never stopped playing spy games. They never stopped fighting the Cold War—they just made us think it was over to trick us into submission. I knew what he was doing the whole time.

DORSET: Do you really think we're still in the midst of the Cold War?

TRUMP: Are there hostilities between our countries still? In some quarters, undoubtedly. So what? I have some hostilities with all my exes. That doesn't mean we can't still show up at the same fundraiser. To meet the challenges of the twenty-first century, Vlad and I need to work together.

DORSET: What type of challenges?

TRUMP: Real bad guys, like the Chinese. ISIS. England.

DORSET: The United Kingdom is the United States' oldest ally. In our recent military endeavors, they've been the one country who we could count on to have our back. Are you suggesting there's some tension between the two countries now?

TRUMP: You tell me. They tried to ban me from their stupid little country, you know.

DORSET: You're referring to the Parliamentary "debate" over whether or not to allow you into the UK, which was triggered by an online petition. Those who signed the petition believed your remarks about Kardashians constituted hate speech.

TRUMP: They're just jealous—not just of me, but of our great country. Their food is terrible. Their sports are terrible. *Bridget Jones* has absolutely nothing on American diaries. I mean, *Gone Girl*—such a superior diary. Way more intrigue. Soccer? We have football. *Real* football. They have James Bond? Say hello to Jason Bourne, who is much better looking. Needs to get laid more, though. You hear about Bond girls. Where are the Bourne girls?

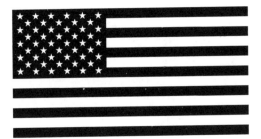

Tuesday, August 28, 2018

CHAPTER SEVENTEEN

★ ★ ★ ★

IN BLOOM

Jimmie woke up in a cold sweat. It was just after four. While he wanted to believe everything Connor had told him was fantasy, his mind was running wild. He'd searched for the GIF Connor had spoken of, the one with the body falling from the White House roof. It appeared to have been all but wiped off the Internet. Thankfully, he found it on a cached Fark link.

It was nothing, really—just a blur. Could have been a gnat flying past the camera lens. No wonder it hadn't taken off. And yet . . . there appeared to be another figure on the roof. Just a shadow. But still . . .

After an hour of tossing and turning, Jimmie gave up on sleep. His brain was on fire with speculation. What *had* happened to Lester Dorset? He dressed and took the Metro to work.

It was still before seven when he arrived at the White House. He decided to stroll the grounds before heading inside. It was too early to hit the slot machines in the Press Room. Plus, he had to see the Rose Garden for himself. He didn't know what he'd find—probably nothing—but he had to see it. He had to see where Connor claimed Lester had met his end, as improbable as it had sounded.

Trump's revamped Rose Garden wrapped around the back of the White House from the East to West Wing. A pair of

Secret Service agents stood at attention near the back doors. Jimmie nodded as he passed them, just to be friendly. They didn't acknowledge his presence. Behind the dark shades, it appeared they were catching some Zs. He thought he heard one snoring.

Even though it was early fall, the garden was still in full bloom. Jimmie couldn't identify any of the flowers besides the roses. He didn't know shit about flowers, except that they were expensive as hell on Valentine's Day and withered to nothing a week later.

Jimmie shot a quick glance up at the third-floor family quarters. The lights were out. Was Trump awake right now, though? Perhaps he was already at breakfast or reading the paper in the Oval Office. The president frequently bragged about how little sleep he got. It didn't sound like something to brag about. It sounded like something to see your doctor about.

A hand drew a curtain to the side. A woman wrapped in a bath towel opened a set of double doors and stepped out onto the third-floor patio. Her wet hair glistened in the dawn's morning light. She was beautiful beyond comparison . . . and she was also the first lady. This was Trump's fifth (but probably not final) wife: Victoria Trump.

She gazed out on the South Lawn, surveying the sand traps and water hazards within her domain.

Jimmie knew he should look away, but he was powerless. He'd never been much of a voyeur. However, it wasn't every day that you saw the first lady step out of the shower. Or maybe it was every day. Maybe if he got here before seven every morning, he could catch a glimpse of the Hottest Wife on the Planet.

That wasn't just in his estimation, either—that was an official title, bestowed by no less an authority than *Maxim* magazine. And it was well deserved. In person, the Latverian model looked even better than she'd looked on *America's Next First Lady*.

Victoria caught sight of Jimmie staring up at her.

He froze in place.

She shot him a knowing smile and slowly undid her towel. Oh so slowly . . .

Just as she was about to show him her first ladies, a light came on behind her. She quickly wrapped the towel back tight around her as her husband approached from behind. He was fully dressed and holding his phone up as if filming video of her. Victoria batted him away and stormed inside. The president shrugged and tapped away on his phone, facing away from Jimmie. A picture of the first lady would pop up on Instagram any second now.

Jimmie's phone chirped in his pocket—the president hadn't posted to social media. He'd sent a group text. Jimmie'd forgotten to switch his phone to silent! Shit.

It chirped again, and Trump swiveled around.

Without thinking, Jimmie dove headfirst into the Rose Garden.

CHAPTER EIGHTEEN

★ ★ ★ ★

ROSES ARE RED, LESTER IS BLUE

If he'd had time to hesitate, Jimmie would have balked at jumping into a flower bed filled with so many roses. Where there were roses, there were thorns. Even a boob like Bret Michaels knew that.

However, as he lay flat on his stomach under the cover of the flower bushes, Jimmie realized he hadn't been scratched. He was going to have to dust the dirt off his suit, but there wasn't a single thorn that had poked him. The flowers were fake. Every single one of them. No wonder the Rose Garden looked so majestic in late August.

Jimmie silenced his phone and rolled over onto his back. Looking up, his eye was drawn to some lettering on the underside of a rose petal: "Made in China." Through the faux foliage, he could see that Trump had disappeared back inside, chasing after Victoria. What the hell had Jimmie been thinking? And more important . . . what the hell had *she* been thinking?

Something scurried through the dirt near him. Before he could even turn his head to check it out, the thing was on his chest.

The first family's dachshund, Opulence, was staring him in the face. It yipped twice, shrill and piercing, then sniffed at his lips. The dog could probably smell the coffee on his breath. If it was looking for food, it would have to look elsewhere—Jimmie had decided to start showing up to work with an empty stomach to avoid any further "incidents."

Opulence turned its attention to the paper bag in Jimmie's hand.

"Not my tuna sandwich," he mumbled. Though, really, what did he care? He was going to get seventy-five bucks every day to spend on food. He was going to pack the pounds on. The dog looked scrawny, and winter was coming.

The skinny wiener dog darted for Jimmie's lunch bag . . . and pushed it out of the way. It started digging in the dirt. Looking for a bone it had buried? Maybe dachshunds weren't into tuna salad.

The dog popped its head back up, and what it had in its mouth was not the bone Jimmie was expecting.

It was a human finger.

A gray, rotted human finger covered in dirt, but a human finger nonetheless.

Jimmie had a good guess whose finger it was even before he saw the gaudy golden ring on it. The inscription encircling the oversized ruby confirmed his suspicions: 1993 PULITZER PRIZE WINNER.

Connor Brent was right. The previous ghostwriter was most certainly dead.

CHAPTER NINETEEN

★ ★ ★ ★

WE DON'T DIAL 9-1-1

EMPLOYEES ONLY. NO TRESPASSING. WE DONT [*sic*] DIAL 9-1-1!

The sign was meant to keep intruders at bay. There was even a little icon of a pistol, in case you were too dim to get the point.

Jimmie, however, wasn't a trespasser. He was a White House employee. He ran his badge over the card reader and heard the door unlock.

He hesitated with his hand on the knob. Despite his obscenely high clearance level, he couldn't entirely be sure he wouldn't be shot on the other side. If he was going to do this, though, he had to move quickly. The White House opened up for tourists in another sixty seconds. He was in one of the most popular rooms: the Reagan Library. The room was stocked with VHS copies of Ronald Reagan's favorite movies—everything from outlaw Westerns to gunfighter Westerns. No books. If there was a single book in the White House outside of Trump's own, Jimmie hadn't seen it yet.

Jimmie slipped through the door. He descended the maintenance staircase on the other side, down into the bowels of the White House. Past the basement . . . and to the subbasement.

There were only two ways to get to the subbasement: via the Reagan Library and via a service elevator in the family quarters. A men's room attendant had advised him to avoid the elevator. It was primarily used by the kitchen staff, who were known to lick. Jimmie didn't ask any other questions. He'd tipped the attendant a twenty for his troubles. Emma thought Jimmie had been in the practice of trading gossip for gossip. He'd been all too happy to not correct her. Cash was frowned upon in the news business, but cash was also king—Trump clearly knew that.

Jimmie pushed open the heavy fire door at the base of the stairs. He was in a walkway lit by what looked like backup lighting. It had that wonderful mid-twentieth-century bomb-shelter aesthetic. All bare concrete walls and exposed metal piping, like a hip coffee shop.

Jimmie was alone in the subbasement.

Uncomfortably alone.

Was the chief janitor's closet down here somewhere? Jimmie had looked at the staff directory, which didn't list a "chief janitor." Whatever Christie was doing at the White House was off the books.

The subbasement seemed like the perfect out-of-the-way place from which to do dirty work. The kind of work that would normally be frowned upon in DC but was commonplace in Jersey. Jimmie hadn't dared ask the men's room attendant any questions about Christie, though. He didn't want the guy to get in any kind of trouble over twenty bucks. God knew people had been killed for less, but still.

Jimmie passed a handful of metal doors, none of which were equipped with electronics for reading badges. He tried one.

Locked. Maybe the subbasement was a dead end—his badge wasn't going to do any good down here.

He turned the corner and paused. There was a door that stood out from the rest, with a *Far Side* cartoon taped to it: A nerd carrying a stack of books was pushing on a door marked "PULL." A sign beside the door read "SCHOOL FOR THE GIFTED."

It smacked of the smarter-than-thou humor a smarmy *New York Times* journalist would find funny.

Jimmie looked both ways and, still finding that he was alone, pressed the handle down. Amazingly, it wasn't locked. He pushed the door open.

Or he tried to. Its hinges were rusted. He tried again, this time throwing his shoulder into it. The door didn't budge, but his spinal column folded like an accordion. Needless to say, the pain was excruciating.

Jimmie stretched his back out. He was about ready to ram the door again when something hit him: The cartoon's subject and placement weren't incidental.

He pressed down on the handle and pulled.

The door opened without difficulty, and he was inside.

CHAPTER TWENTY

★ ★ ★ ★

CLOSE ENOUGH FOR GOVERNMENT WORK

With the flip of a switch, a long, single-bulb fluorescent light hanging from the ceiling flickered on. The room was set up as an office—the world's smallest office, but an office nonetheless. There was barely enough room for two people to stand side by side in front of the metal desk, which stretched from bare wall to bare wall. There was a filing cabinet on the other side of the desk, but there didn't appear to be any way to get to it. A chair back poked up from behind the desk. It wasn't ergonomic; it was a torture device.

"I see you've found your new office."

Jimmie spun around. Emma was standing in the doorway, arms folded.

"Thought I'd do a little snooping around," he stammered.

"You're free to go wherever you please," she said. "Sorry that the office is a little on the small side, but it's all we have left."

"I used to live in Manhattan," Jimmie said. "This looks like a penthouse suite compared to some of my old apartments."

"Fascinating," she said.

"You think I'm exaggerating?"

"No," she said. "It's fascinating that you think I care."

It was taking her a while to warm up to him. The president had probably chewed her ear off regarding the elevator incident yesterday, so Jimmie couldn't exactly blame her for being so chilly. At least he still had a job. That was really all that mattered. He was beyond caring what beautiful women thought of him.

Emma asked, "Do you have your tux for the State Dinner this evening?"

"The steak dinner?"

"*State* Dinner," she said, obviously annoyed he hadn't read the e-mail with the president's schedule. Hey, at least he hadn't deleted it. "The president and Putin are out hunting together right now. Festivities start at six."

"Tux. Already rented. Gotta pick it up after lunch."

She stared at him for a beat, seeing through his lie but not calling him on it. He appreciated that in a boss. He figured he could trust her. He was going to have to trust somebody around here, and she hadn't batted an eye when she'd found him snooping downstairs.

"The first biographer," he blurted out. "The man who had this office before me . . . Lester Dorset. He's not backpacking the Pacific Crest Trail, is he?"

She shook her head. "He's never even read *Wild*. This isn't public knowledge, but . . . he took his own life. It was a great shock to everyone," she said, her voice no more than a hushed whisper. "Climbed onto the roof and jumped . . . right into the Rose Garden."

"Jesus." Jimmie couldn't say much else. Because what do you say when you hear something like that? A coworker kills themselves on the job? In the springtime, when you saw the fake flowers blooming, how could you not think about a body lying there?

And yet . . . Jimmie had to press further.

"You sure he jumped? He wasn't . . . pushed?"

"I was right about you," Emma said.

"That I've got a nose for a story?"

"That you're still living in your dirt-sheet fantasy world," she said. "It's just your second day on the job, and you're already snooping around for scandals. This is one story you can forget about, though. Not many people have roof access. Who was going to push him off? Surely not the president or the first lady, who were in Mar-a-Lago for the Fourth of July. There's no story here."

Except there is a body, Jimmie thought. *And where there's a body, there's a story. If somebody kills themselves, you don't just dig a hole in the backyard and throw them in. That's what you do if somebody is murdered.*

He remembered from that boring Watergate movie how upset people got when Nixon lied about the break-in at the Democratic National headquarters. The *Washington Post* had won a Pulitzer for that dull bit of reporting!

Imagine, now, if there'd been a dead body involved.

Whoever reported that story wouldn't just win a Pulitzer— they'd win an Edgar from the Mystery Writers of America. They'd win their girl back. If that was something they were theoretically hoping to do, which he wasn't.

Lester was dead, but somebody was lying. Too bad the dog had made off with the evidence, but he guessed there was more where that came from. Jimmie Bernwood was going to find out the killer's identity . . . if he lived long enough.

If anyone *lived long enough,* he thought, remembering what Connor had said about the war with the United Kingdom— and the potentially looming threat of World War III.

CHAPTER TWENTY-ONE

★ ★ ★ ★

CANDY IS DANDY, BUT LIQUOR IS QUICKER

After Emma left, Jimmie pulled his White House–issued phone out to find a tux rental shop nearby. "Find men's wear stores," he instructed his phone.

"Sorry, I didn't hear you," his phone said in that bitchy voice of hers. "Please speak up."

He cleared his throat. "FIND MEN'S WEAR STORES!"

There was a click above his head. Jimmie looked up. There was nothing above him but the ceiling. Rats? Not in the Trump White House. *That click sounded familiar*, he thought, climbing onto his desk. He pushed aside a tile and reached around until—

There. He pulled the device out. A Tascam DR-08 Portable Digital Recorder. It was voice activated, which explained why it had clicked on when he'd shouted. It wouldn't record conversations very well through the tile, though, so he doubted someone had placed it up there to record him. Chris Christie and whomever else was in charge of eavesdropping at the White House probably had much more advanced ways of bugging rooms. No, this had been hidden in the ceiling. He was as sure of it as he'd been sure of anything in his life. Which is to say, not a hundred percent sure. But, as he'd heard around the West Wing, "close enough for government work."

Jimmie turned his phone off and pressed PLAY on the recorder.

Let's start at the beginning. You were born in 19—

That's not how you're going to begin the book, is it? With my head poking out of my mother's wherever?

With your birth? Not necessarily, but that's basically how Dickens started David Copperfield.

Even more reason not to do it. I hate magicians.

The first voice was Lester's. The second was Trump's. The interview sessions recorded by Lester Dorset existed after all. They weren't tapes, however—they were on a hard drive embedded into the recorder. The security measure Emma had talked about. Connor Brent's insane story about evidence that would lead to Trump's downfall was no Bernie bro fantasy.

Jimmie was tempted to listen to the recordings now, but he couldn't. He returned the recorder to its hiding spot. Right now, he had to find a fly tux. His afternoon was booked already, too—the bathroom attendant had invited him to play Cards Against Humility with some of the blue-collar staff in the breakroom.

After that, it would be time to hit the State Dinner. Where they might not have steak, but they would sure as shit have some booze. Anything less would be a middle finger to the Russian president. Perhaps someone would drop a few more hints about what really happened to Lester Dorset. Cash was great for getting people to cough up information, but alcohol was better.

CHAPTER TWENTY-TWO

★ ★ ★ ★

STRAWBERRY
AND CINNAMON

Trump and Putin descended the Grand Staircase, preceded by a phalanx of flag-bearing Marines. The crowd, including Jimmie, clapped enthusiastically at the president's arrival. "The President's Own" US Marine Band segued from "America the Beautiful" into a brass rendition of Twisted Sister's "We're Not Gonna Take It."

The world leaders waved from the first step as the flashbulbs went off.

Putin stepped to the microphone. "I thank the Donald for his invitation and affirm that we, Russia, stand by our friend, America, against her enemies around the world . . . especially if they have limp wrists and posh accents."

When Trump took the mic, Jimmie slipped out to the State Dining Room. He wanted to get a good seat. Someplace close to the buffet, so he could load up his plate before John Kasich hit it. Kasich was already creeping toward the door in the most wrinkled tuxedo Jimmie had ever seen. Rumor had it the poor guy was living in his car.

Not only wasn't there a buffet, however, but it turned out he hadn't needed to rush: The seating was assigned. Emma had put Jimmie at the head-of-state table right next to Trump and Putin.

Good. Excellent, in fact. Vladimir Putin was at the top of Jimmie's list of suspects for Lester's murder.

Jimmie had visited the WhiteHouse.gov website and found the list of everyone who'd been at the White House the night of July fourth. While the Trumps had indeed been out of town, three people besides Lester had clearance levels that would have given them access to the roof: Chris Christie, Corey Lewandowski, and—staying in the Lincoln Bedroom as a guest of the White House—Russian president Vladimir Putin. There'd been a handful of Secret Service agents with free rein of the family quarters and access to the roof. However, as Jimmie had seen, the Secret Service seemed to have no interest in lifting a finger for Trump. They weren't going to kill somebody to protect his reputation. They wouldn't even shoot somebody in the kneecaps.

After a half hour, Trump finally arrived in the dining room and took a seat next to Jimmie. "If you're going to puke tonight, do it on the press," the president told him.

"I'll see what I can do," Jimmie said, a bit too enthusiastically. He'd been back and forth to the open bar a couple of times already. He had a decent buzz going.

"Have you been to one of these things before?" Trump asked Jimmie.

"Politics isn't my usual beat," he said. "But I've had dinner before."

"You're going to love it. You're going to have an amazing, amazing time. Do you know Vlad?"

Jimmie shook his head and self-consciously pulled the sleeves of his tuxedo jacket down. There hadn't been time for alterations, so he was wearing a tux two sizes too small.

"Vlad is a riot," Trump said. "We were out hunting today. Oh, boy. That guy, I tell you what."

Jimmie could see it now: Trump, a big proponent of the Second Amendment, and Putin, an avid outdoorsman, marching through the Virginia woods together, blasting deer with Uzis.

"Will the first lady be joining us tonight?" Jimmie asked.

Trump snorted. "She hates Vlad. Thinks he's a bad influence on me. Every time we get together, I end up stumbling home at four in the morning smelling like Strawberry and Cinnamon. And I'm not talking about scents. I'm talking about dancers. Those are their names: Strawberry and Cinnamon."

"I get it," Jimmie said.

"Good. You're a good guy. You got a weak stomach, but you're a good guy."

"Thank you, Mr. President."

"Please—call me Trump. There've been how many presidents? Forty? Fifty? There's only one Trump."

Unless you counted his wives, or his parents, or his children. But Jimmie had a feeling Trump didn't count them.

"We have to schedule a time to talk," Trump continued. "You've got to see the Oval Office. You know that it's really an oval?"

"I was never any good at geometry," Jimmie said, scanning the dining room. More than a hundred guests were seated and chatting, waiting on the arrival of the Russian president. Jimmie was already starting to sweat under the opulent chandeliers, which cast so much light that it felt like he was in a tanning bed. Perhaps that was how Trump kept his luxurious glow intact.

"Which one of my hotels did Emma put you up in?" Trump asked.

"I found a place on my own. You know the Royal Linoleum?"

"Are you trying to get yourself killed?" Trump said. "I'll talk to Emma. We'll set you up in one of my properties."

Jimmie chose his words carefully. "If there happens to be an advertised vacancy at a Trump building, of course, I'll jump on it. I don't want any special treatment."

"A vacant unit in a Trump building is about as rare as a Kate Winslet movie where we don't see her honkers," Trump said. "But I see your point. You're a man who likes to do things on his own. You don't like to be dependent on others. I can respect that. Can I give you some advice, though?"

Jimmie nodded.

"Until you can move out of the shithole where you're living, stay away from Clinton Plaza. It's a dangerous place. A dangerous, dangerous place. All sorts of degenerates there. I'm not just talking about the homeless or the marijuana addicts, either. There are dangerous people with dangerous ideas." Trump leaned closer. "You understand what I'm saying?"

Jimmie sipped his water. Suddenly, his throat had gone very dry.

CHAPTER TWENTY-THREE

★ ★ ★

TRUMP ZERO

Before Jimmie could respond to what sounded an awful lot like a veiled threat, Vladimir Putin slapped Trump hard on the back.

Trump swung around, fists at the ready to defend himself. When he saw who it was, though, he jumped up to greet his buddy.

Putin put Trump in a playful headlock, and the American president threw up his arms in mock protest. The Secret Service agent with the shaved head—the one Jimmie had met the day before under very different circumstances—stood back a few feet, watching the public display of affection. Step aside, Patrick Stewart and Ian McKellen—there was a new bromance in town.

Jimmie wondered how much Trump/Putin slash fic there was out there. It wasn't a question of whether or not it existed but a question of how many shippers had avoided legal trouble from Trump's team.

A nervous waiter carefully poured a Miller Lite into a chilled glass for the Russian president, who had taken a seat on the other side of Trump. Putin made a hand gesture to a tuxedoed man who'd accompanied him into the dining room. KGB, Jimmie guessed. If that was still a thing.

The KGB agent swished a light swig of the beer around in his mouth. He had an intense look of concentration, which was made all the more intense by the scar bisecting his right eye. He swallowed and gave Putin a sharp nod. The Russian president shot a perplexed Trump a look that said, *You can never be too careful.*

The waiter poured a Trump Zero for the president, who then held his glass out to the Secret Service agent behind him.

The agent made no move for the glass. Jimmie imagined he was rolling his eyes behind his shades, which he was wearing indoors simply to hide his annoyance with Trump.

Not wishing to be outdone on his own turf, Trump swung the glass around to Jimmie, who had no choice but to reluctantly accept it.

Jimmie cradled the glass with two hands and put it to his own lips, as if he were about to drink from the Holy Grail. He took a healthy swig and tried to repeat the KGB agent's performance, swishing the carbonated liquid around like mouthwash. Had it been tampered with? How would he know? Unlike Putin's goon, Jimmie was no poison sommelier. He tried to think back to the last time he'd even had a poisoned drink. When was that? Oh, yeah: way back in NINETEEN NINETY-NEVER.

Still, he made an attempt. What struck him at first was just how much like regular Trump Cola it tasted. Jimmie didn't drink much pop. When he did, he usually opted for the stuff with real sugar or corn sweetener—the good stuff, in other words. Diet pop just tasted so phony, with that metallic aftertaste. He'd seen Trump Zero advertised as a better-tasting zero-calorie beverage, but it had always seemed too good to be true.

What a fool he'd been.

What a goddamned fool.

Jimmie handed the glass back to Trump, who raised his eyebrows expectantly. Putin leaned forward, craning his neck

89

around Trump. The room itself seemed to be holding its breath, waiting upon his pronouncement.

Jimmie finally gave a single nod, prompting a collective sigh of relief from the room.

After the taste test, Trump and Putin settled into a rowdy back-and-forth. At first, Jimmie tried leaning in to pick up as much of their conversation as he could, but Putin shot him an annoyed look. Jimmie backed off. Although he'd been seated close so that he could eavesdrop with impunity, he didn't want to raise the Russian president's ire. After all, Putin may have thrown the last ghostwriter off the White House roof to protect Trump.

Corey Lewandowski was seated to Jimmie's left. Another possible suspect. Lewandowski was locked into a heated conversation with Secretary of State Omarosa over whether they should call the United Kingdom "England" or "Great Britain." Jimmie had no interest in joining them, however. Lewandowski had already punched one waiter in the nuts for not refilling his water fast enough. And Omarosa . . . well, Jimmie remembered her from the first season of *The Apprentice*. He had no interest in tangling horns with her. He was referring, of course, to the literal horns that had sprouted from her forehead. Once, she'd shaved them down, but these days they grew long and curled.

Chris Christie, who was sitting directly across from Jimmie, made a gun with his hand. He pointed his index finger directly at Jimmie and pressed his thumb down. *BANG.* The White House janitor returned to his plate of cheese sticks, leaving Jimmie to wonder just what the hell kind of mess he'd gotten himself into this time. He was seated at a table with the most powerful men and women in the world . . . one of whom was a killer.

CHAPTER TWENTY-FOUR

★ ★ ★ ★

WWTDYL

Before the State Dinner, the best meal of Jimmie Bernwood's life had been at the Marriott Marquis Hotel in downtown Atlanta.

Cat, whom he was sort of dating at the time, was in Atlanta at one of those week-long journalism conferences. The kind with all the panels and workshops. Not Jimmie's bag, but whatever.

By day three on his own in New York, however, he'd run out of packaged food in his apartment and had wicked-smart blisters on his hands. From, uh, playing video games. Why not surprise his girl by driving thirteen hours straight and showing up at her hotel unannounced? A grand, romantic gesture.

When Jimmie arrived at her hotel room, she'd answered the door in a robe, giggling deliriously. She looked at him first with confusion and then second with more confusion.

"Hurry up, babe," a man's voice said from inside the hotel room. Jimmie could see a pair of naked feet on the bed, just over Cat's bare shoulder. The naked, wrinkled feet . . . of a naked, wrinkled man. The hair on the back of Jimmie's neck stood up. It was the hetero Spidey-sense every straight guy possesses that lets him know there's an exposed penis in close proximity.

"I'm sorry," Cat whispered. "I thought you were—"

"In New York?" Jimmie said.

She shook her head. "I thought you were room service."

He could have given her a chance to explain herself, but what was going on seemed pretty self-explanatory. He could also have pushed her aside and confronted whoever she was sleeping with, but he didn't know if he could control his anger. He was sure he would learn who the man was eventually (and he was right—it was that Pulitzer-winning prick, Lester Dorset).

Jimmie stumbled backward, awkwardly, and then sprinted down the hall to the elevators. When the elevator door opened, a bellhop pushed a food cart out the door.

"Room 1273?" Jimmie said.

The bellhop nodded.

"I'm taking it to go," Jimmie said, shoving the cart back into the elevator. He pushed the CLOSE DOOR button and waved to the stunned bellhop as the elevator doors shuttered. Jimmie lifted the lid off one of the food trays. Salmon and rice. Not bad. He hadn't eaten a thing since his journalist power lunch, which consisted of a banana and a hard-boiled egg swiped from coworkers' lunch bags.

He uncorked the pinot grigio that had been resting in the wine chiller and drank and drank and drank some more, riding the elevator up and down, up and down until he was thrown out of the hotel.

That was a good meal.

The State Dinner, however, was giving that stolen room-service meal some serious competition. The White House chef, Guy Fieri, had prepared an array of appetizers, culled from the finest fast-food joints in the DC area. They'd all provided the food gratis for the free advertising. No president had ever had sponsorship deals in place with fast-food restaurants before, but the United States had never seen a president like Donald J. Trump before. It was all quite practical—and, dare to say, somewhat genius.

For Jimmie, the best part was that it was all on the house. He wasn't expected to tip the waitstaff even 10 percent. The White House was taking care of the bill.

No, scratch that. The best part was when he spotted Cat Diaz seated at one of the press tables . . . and then she spotted him sitting next to the world's two most powerful leaders.

Jimmie raised his Miller Lite to her from across the room in a mock toast. He thought about dialing his smirk down a notch or two but couldn't bring himself to do it. It was like those bracelets, the ones they sold in the White House gift shop: *WWTDYL? (What Would Trump Do, You Loser?)*. When Trump won—which he did often—he let people know about it. "If you don't talk about your successes, nobody's going to know about them," Trump wrote in the expanded coloring book edition of *Trump: The Art of the Deal*, which Jimmie had only colored a quarter of the way through. "And if nobody knows about your successes, then you haven't really won, have you?"

Jimmie puckered his lips and threw a smooch Cat's way.

She rolled her eyes and looked away in disgust.

Hashtag: WINNING.

CHAPTER TWENTY-FIVE

★ ★ ★ ★

PANDA EXPRESS

"It's good to be king," Trump said, startling Jimmie. The president had seen his little back-and-forth with Cat.

"*President,*" Jimmie said. "Don't you mean, *It's good to be president?*"

"Same difference."

A trio of waiters rolled carts up to their table. The main course had arrived: burgers. Trump's favorite food. Distinctly American.

Unlike the rest of the appetizers and side dishes that had been rolled out, the burgers weren't served in fast-food wrappers. The burgers stood half a foot tall, with buns the size of Trump's ego. The meat bleeding onto the plates had to weigh at least a half pound. At least. And the smell . . . the smell was so invigorating that Jimmie had to shift the napkin in his lap because of how hard it made him.

The KGB agent stepped in to sample Putin's burger. Jimmie eyed Trump's plate, awaiting an order to do likewise.

"Touch my burger, and I cut your fingers off," Trump snapped. "No joke, buckaroo."

Jimmie dug his teeth into his own burger, tearing off a chunk like a velociraptor tearing into the belly of a just-felled triceratops.

"This . . . is . . . wow," he said while chewing. What few manners he had had completely gone out the window. "Trump Steak?"

"Panda Express," Putin said, causing Trump to giggle with a full mouth.

Panda Express didn't serve burgers, as far as Jimmie knew. Then again, when you were the president of the most powerful nation in the world, you could probably call in a few favors from your friends in the fast-food industry. Maybe they'd made MSG burgers, just for the State Dinner.

Putin took a sip of beer. "I kill it myself. You like?"

Jimmie nodded. "Venison?"

A look of confusion crossed Putin's face.

"Deer," Jimmie said. "From when you guys went hunting today?"

"Panda," Putin said. "Is panda. Is most challenging animal to track since they sleep so much."

"You have pandas in Russia?"

Putin shook his head. "You have pandas here. In zoo. We go hunting at zoo."

Jimmie stared at the burger in his hands. Red juice ran down his palms and dripped onto the plate.

He'd visited the National Zoo a couple of years back. Which of the giant pandas was he eating right now? Tian Tian? Mei Xiang? Bao Bao? Or—God forbid—the cute-as-a-button cub, Bei Bei? Any of them but Bei Bei!

Jimmie looked around the room at the packed tables. The State Dinner guests were busy gnashing their way unawares through panda burgers. It would be a miracle if Trump and Putin had left a single giant panda alive at the National Zoo. It would be a miracle if they'd left *any* animal alive. How they'd let Trump and Putin stalk and kill caged animals was beyond him. Diplomatic immunity, perhaps?

The first lady was right to be distrustful of Putin. The man was a bad influence on Trump. How much of the talk about "going for a three-peat against England" was just Trump trying to impress his BFF? Was the Russian president influencing the American president in even more direct ways . . . advising him, perhaps? Had this clearly dangerous man thrown Lester off the roof so that they could continue beating the war drums together?

Jimmie set the burger down. The thought of eating one of the last two thousand pandas in the world disgusted him. He couldn't bring himself to finish the burger.

However, he couldn't let it go to waste, either.

He flagged down a passing waiter. "Could I get a to-go box for this?"

CHAPTER TWENTY-SIX

★ ★ ★ ★

CHECK, PLEASE

Jimmie glanced in the direction of Clinton Plaza as he stepped off the bus. Had the president known about his little clandestine meeting last night? Unlikely. The "dangerous people with dangerous ideas" could have been the Occupy protestors who camped out in the park when the weather was nice enough. If the president had known about his midnight meeting, Jimmie would surely have been fired by now.

Or worse.

As Jimmie turned the doorknob to his room, he noticed the frame was splintered around the lock. It hadn't been damaged this morning.

He pushed the door open slowly, holding the key out like a knife. It was the only weapon he had on him. He hoped the key might catch the streetlight and appear to be a weapon in his hand.

"I've got a knife," Jimmie announced, peering into the darkness. Then as an afterthought, "And a gun."

Why not add some nunchucks to that list while you're at it, genius?

There was no response from inside the room, save for the sound of his own voice rattling around his head. He flipped the light switch on.

The room was empty. There was no assassin in the bathroom. Ditto with the shower and the closet and underneath the queen-size bed.

His laptop was still under the pile of soiled laundry. Nothing had been stolen. Maybe somebody had opened his laptop—maybe they'd hacked into it—but why not just take it? While there were unanswered questions, he had no doubt that someone had been in his room. Somebody besides the cleaning staff.

He ran down the list of suspects. While Putin had been with Trump all day, he could have sent one of his KGB goons over to do the dirty work. Corey Lewandowski could have snuck away from the White House at any point during the day, though it seemed unlikely with his busy schedule. Chris Christie? Yeah, that sounded about right. A little B and E seemed right up the White House janitor's alley.

The Socialist Justice Warriors could have also been upset he rejected their offer. They could have come for his laptop, looking for evidence of presidential wrongdoing on it. If so, they were pissing up the wrong tree. Jimmie knew better than to access his work e-mail from his home computer. He didn't want to pull a Hillary.

Regardless of who the culprit was, the Royal Linoleum Hotel was no longer safe. If it ever had been.

✯ ✯ ✯ ✯

Excerpt From the Trump/Dorset Sessions

June 1, 2018, 10:16 AM

DORSET: Before you decided to run for president, you were a larger-than-life presence in Manhattan and

Atlantic City real estate, as well as on television screens with *The Apprentice* and *The Celebrity Apprentice*.

TRUMP: And let's not forget Trump Resorts all over the world. I had my own magazine, my own water. I had my own steaks, sold through the Sharper Image catalog. Who did that before Donald Trump? Nobody. They all told me it was a stupid idea. Now, everybody orders meat through the mail. If you go into a grocery store to buy steak, they'll look at you like you're a dummy. You buy it through Amazon now, and a drone drops it off thirty minutes later directly onto your grill.

DORSET: It's interesting that you would bring up Amazon, what with all the animosity in the past between you and Jeff Bezos's newspaper, the *Washington Post*—though they've been surprisingly gentle on you during your first term in office.

TRUMP: He's a businessman, I'm a businessman. If there's a deal to be made, I'll make it. Bezos asked me to loosen the restrictions on commercial drone usage, and I asked him to call off the *Post*. So we made a deal.

DORSET: A lot of people would consider it unethical for the president of the United States to be trading favors for relaxing government regulations.

TRUMP: Unethical? Who's using that word? I've never taken a dime from anyone in exchange for influence. I don't need their money. I'm very wealthy. This is two consenting adults agreeing to a mutually beneficial situation. That's never unethical.

DORSET: Surely you've seen tweets to this effect. Twitter seems to be rife with critics of the administration. There are entire parody accounts—

TRUMP: Illegal parody accounts. I've had many of them shut down. You can't impersonate a sitting president. Can't do it. So I have my lawyers get on them.

DORSET: There's actually a Supreme Court precedent that says it's legal: Hustler Magazine v. Falwell. If a reasonable person wouldn't interpret a parody to be true—if it's clearly a mockery, in other words—then it's covered by the First Amendment.

TRUMP: Who's reasonable? You? Most people aren't logical. I'm talking mostly about women, but I know plenty of men who can be really bitchy.

DORSET: Fair enough. But you have to admit that nobody would mistake @WriteinTrump for the real thing. Here's a sample tweet—again, clearly not something you've ever said: "I'm not willing to say that I'm one hundred percent sure O. J. Simpson committed those murders until I know where Obama was that night."

TRUMP: Well, where *was* Obama that night?

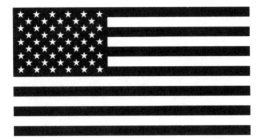

Wednesday, August 29, 2018

CHAPTER TWENTY-SEVEN

✯ ✯ ✯ ✯

SAY CHEESE!

The first thing Jimmie did when he arrived at his office the next morning was push his desk up against the door and open the ceiling tile. He breathed a sigh of relief—temporary relief, but relief nonetheless. Lester's recorder was still there.

Too bad he couldn't just smuggle it out of the White House. Not with the insane, paranoid security in place. He could, however, listen to the taped interviews when he had the opportunity.

Not now, however. He'd just received an e-mail that an emergency meeting had been called for nine o'clock. No dessert this time, from the sound of things.

Jimmie slipped through the door at the top of the stairs and into the Reagan Library. A group of tourists stared at him, bewildered expressions on their faces. A couple of them raised their phones, snapping photos. They probably thought he was somebody important. Let 'em. It wasn't every day you saw a sharp-dressed man slip out from behind a door marked EMPLOYEES ONLY.

Jimmie straightened his tie. He raised an eyebrow—slowly, slyly. *Take all the pictures you want.* If anyone posted pics of him online, it might drive some chatter in certain circles. There were probably shots from the State Dinner floating around, too. Although he wasn't allowed to discuss his project with others, anyone with half a brain would figure out shortly that he was back—in a big way. And working on something bigger than anything he'd ever worked on before. Maybe something even bigger than a ghostwriting project, if this Lester Dorset situation yielded a juicy story.

"Is this great or what?" Trump whispered in his ear. He was standing behind Jimmie, smiling and waving to the tourists. They'd been trying to snap the president's photograph. Jimmie, primping and preening for their cameras, was nothing more than a photobomb.

"Good morning, Mr. Trump," Jimmie said. He tried not to think about his face going fifty shades of red. He wanted to ask how the president and the Secret Service agent just behind him had slipped so silently into the room. He hadn't heard them clanging on the ancient staircase. Presidential teleporter, maybe? Naw—teleportation was an impossibility, even according to the nuttiest professors.

After Trump signed a couple of babies, they moved through the long hallway and into the West Wing.

Jimmie said, "About your offer last night . . ."

"I knew it wouldn't be long. I'll set you up in the best place—one of my favorite properties. Close to here, too. The Watergate. Ever hear of it?"

"Yeah. There was break-in there. Years ago. It was made into a movie."

"Haven't seen it," Trump said. "The hotel is beautiful now. Amazing place. Luxurious. You'll love what I've done with it."

Trump didn't seem able to leave anything well enough alone. Once he got his hands on something, he remade it in his own image.

Jimmie wondered if *he* was getting a Trump makeover. He was already wearing a suit and tie to work. In college, he'd told his roommate that if he ever got a job that required a tie, to strangle him with it and drag his body to the curb to be taken out with the trash.

Now Jimmie was going to be living in a Trump building. How long before he started tanning and turned the color of Cheetos dust? How long before he grew his thinning hair long enough to comb it over his receding hairline in the Trumpster's signature style?

He looked at himself in a passing mirror and tried to smile, but all he could do was smirk.

It was already happening.

CHAPTER TWENTY-EIGHT

★ ★ ★ ★

BOOMTOWN

Trump swaggered into the Tyson Room and headed straight to his seat. Jimmie headed for the corner, where he tried to look invisible by sucking his gut in.

"All right, guys, what is it?" Trump said. "This better be important. I was midbronzing all the way down in the subbasement."

The cabinet members looked around anxiously. Finally, it was Secretary of State Omarosa who spoke.

"The United Kingdom seems to be preparing for an escalation."

Trump snorted. "What are we talking about? Another insult? These guys are terrible at insults."

"No—this time they've taken actual action."

"What, like recalling their ambassador or something?"

Omarosa shook her head. "They've recalled Patrick Stewart. Also Emily Blunt and Andrew Lincoln."

"Aw, crap," interjected the secretary of transportation, Clint Eastwood. "That means no more *Walking Dead*. I gotta find out what happens to Daryl!"

"Just read the comic books," grumbled Corey Lewandowski.

"Why don't *you* read the comic books?" snarled Eastwood with such a menacing tone that Lewandowski paled and became very interested in his glass of water. Jimmie made a mental note to bring that moment up the next time Lewandowski got in his face (not that Jimmie would do any better if he got a full blast of Eastwood).

"So what?" Trump shrugged. "Let the Brits go crawling back to their fog and their bars that close at eleven."

"Bringing their citizens home means they expect things to turn violent," said Omarosa.

"They're damn right it's about to get violent!" said Secretary of Defense Nugent. "Just give the word, boss, and it's boomtown at Buckingham Place."

"This is not an emergency, folks," said Trump. "What have any of those people actually done lately? Nada, except for that *Walking Dead* guy, and nobody knows he's British. I didn't find out until my first security briefing. These guys think this gives them leverage on us? They got nothing. They're running scared."

Now Chris Christie piped in. "You let me know what airports these guys are flying out of. I can make sure it's a looong time before they actually make it across the pond."

"LAX, most likely. Hartsfield for Andrew Lincoln," said Eastwood.

Christie was already speed-dialing a number on his cell. "LAX and ATL. The full Fort Lee," he said, then hung up. He looked at Trump. "It's done."

For no reason that Jimmie could figure, Christie then stared right at him with a look that said, *You're next.*

"Let's get the word out that these guys think they're too good for us," Trump said to Lewandowski. "Get into the next news cycle before the queen gets a chance to give her own reason.

Let me know if it looks like they're actually getting their message out, and I'll call Michelle Obama an ugg-o or something, drown them out."

"Done," said Lewandowski.

"Hey, can we do something really nice for the French?" asked Trump. "That'll really get under their pale English skin."

"I'll get my staff on it," said Omarosa.

"All right, enough of those guys. Is that it?"

"The governor of Kansas has finally called, looking for disaster funding to clean up after last week's tornados," Emma said.

"Does he want the standard relief package or the Trump Premium Plan?" asked Trump.

"What's the premium plan?" Jimmie whispered to the assistant next to him.

"Standard, we help them rebuild. Premium, they get a Trump office complex on the demolished site of their choice," she whispered back.

Emma checked her iPad and replied, "He's leaning Premium. But I think we can talk him up to the Trump Executive Level."

"Let's do it," said Trump. "Remind him if they license a second casino, we throw in a free school. Other business, or are we done?"

"Iran has turned away the UN's nuclear inspectors again," said Omarosa.

"Iran's a nobody," said Trump. "Do they honestly think they can get a nuke? They can't have a nuke. Nuge, where are we at over there?"

"I got seventy-five drones within two hundred miles of Tehran," said the secretary of defense. "We got guys in the satellite room sitting there, waiting, watching. Tracking their habits. We know where they hide their glow sticks, all right. Just say the word, and that place will be glowing so bright, *Egypt* won't be able to sleep."

Note to self, Jimmie thought. *Stay on Ted Nugent's good side.*

"All right, let's do that thing where we talk to the guy who talks to the guy who talks to the guy who tells Ayatollah what's-his-name that he lets the inspectors back in or we're gonna light up the sky like the Fourth of July. No—wait. Like Christmas. That'll piss those Kardashians off even more," Trump said, rubbing his hands together eagerly. "Oh, that is beautiful. I love that plan. You know what else? I love having drones. I see why Obama used them so much now."

"Death from above," intoned Ted Nugent.

"And I want to keep on top of the England thing," Trump said. "Let's find one British guy who's an American citizen—maybe that Craig Ferguson guy—and get him to stay here. He says he picks us over them, I give him an exclusive interview or something."

"I think he's Scottish," said Emma.

"Same difference, right? Or do they have more problems than we thought? Hang on a second." Trump pulled out his phone and typed a tweet as he spoke it aloud: "If England's so great, why is Scotland trying to break up with them all the time? England has nothing to offer! Hashtag LOSERS!"

"Good one, boss," said Chris Christie.

"All right, good meeting. Let's get somebody on some T-shirt designs for the party when the British surrender," Trump said. What followed next was an unholy, jarring noise like a macaw choking—a noise that, Jimmie realized, was Trump laughing.

CHAPTER TWENTY-NINE

✯ ✯ ✯ ✯

TWELVE ANGRY MEN

As the meeting slowly dispersed, Jimmie picked up the *Washington Post* off the pile of newspapers on the meeting-room table. The front-page stories were all about Vice President Tom Brady's trip to the new American moon base. He'd been shot into space the previous week. His mission was scheduled to last through the week of the midterm elections. (The jokes about whether he could keep his space suit inflated had started months earlier and hadn't let up.) It was almost as if somebody wanted the VP out of the country. Way out of the country.

Jimmie glanced at the *Post*'s review of the all-female remake of *Twelve Angry Men*, which was still called *Twelve Angry Men*. He read the score of the Nationals game. They were on a roll. Probably headed to the World Series.

He turned to the Metro section. The top local headline read, "You'll Never Guess Which Georgetown Rowing Star Was Killed in a Military Training Exercise Gone Wrong."

Jimmie was about to skip to the next headline when the photo caught his eye.

Jimmie did a double take, and then a triple take. The blond hair . . . the high cheekbones . . . the Millennial smirk . . . There was no mistaking it: The photo of the Georgetown student identified as David Connor Brent was the same Connor Brent he'd met in the park two nights ago.

Brent had been rowing solo on the Potomac last night when he rowed straight into a naval training exercise. A Navy SEAL platoon was in the middle of a simulated attack using live rounds. Buoys labeled CAUTION had apparently been floating nearby to warn boats away. It wasn't known why David Connor Brent had rowed past them, but he had been reduced to chum in a matter of seconds.

Strangest damn "accident" Jimmie had ever heard of.

Jimmie tried to keep his reaction in check, but it was impossible. It felt like he'd just been slugged in the wedding tackle.

"Everything okay?" Emma asked. "You look like you've seen a ghost."

Jimmie folded the paper and slid it back to the middle of the table. He looked her straight in the eye. "Harper left yesterday's game with a sprained ankle. Even if he stays off the DL, I'm looking at three to five games without his bat in the lineup on my fantasy team."

Emma rolled her eyes at him. For a second there, Jimmie had thought she'd been on to him. It seemed apparent to him that if she'd had any involvement in Brent's death, it would have shown on her face.

Hers weren't the only eyes on him, though—there were others lingering in the room, watching his reaction. Corey Lewandowski had been foaming at the mouth as Jimmie read the article. It was possible the press secretary had rabies. Had there been any bite marks on Lester's body? Jimmie didn't know. All he knew was that the game had just gotten deadlier.

Twice as deadly, to be precise.

CHAPTER THIRTY

★ ★ ★ ★

BIEBS

DORSET: You've had some issues with women in the past.

TRUMP: No one's a greater supporter of women than me. I love women. My mother was a woman—a great woman.

DORSET: I'm thinking, specifically, of your Twitter war with Helen Mirren. You retweeted somebody calling her a "bimbo."

TRUMP: I never called her that. I would never call a woman a "bimbo." Never. Who calls women names like that? It's juvenile.

DORSET: Okay. You have called her "crazy," though.

TRUMP: Well, yeah. If she's acting like some kind of crazy bimbo, I'm going to call her crazy.

DORSET: Did . . . you just call her a bimbo?

TRUMP: Don't twist my words. Do not twist my words. I never said she was a crazy bimbo. I said she was acting like a crazy bimbo. Take your dick out of your ear and listen to what I'm saying.

Jimmie reached the end of the recordings. He'd spent the past five hours holed up in his office listening to Lester's interviews . . . all for nothing.

Jimmie could see why Lester Dorset thought there were some "game-changing" admissions on the hard drive. Trump spoke candidly with Lester Dorset about buying favor in the media. He called the Mighty Mississippi a "river of slime" running through the United States. At one point, he even referred to the Second Amendment as one of the Ten Commandments. Lester, the golden boy for the country's most liberal rag, had to have shit himself at that one!

The problem was that Lester Dorset had always been an idealist. A fool who believed in the essential goodness of the American people. Lester probably thought that if he could expose the man behind the orange mask, the people would come to their senses and storm the gates.

Unfortunately, Jimmie knew better. Trump was what those on the celebrity-gossip beat called a "Biebs." No matter what you wrote about Justin Bieber in the dirt sheets, he still managed to top the iTunes charts. Trump was the same way. He could do wheelies on a motorbike over Ronald Reagan's grave, and half the country would still vote for him in 2020.

While many of Trump's admissions were indeed eye raising, none of them were "game changing."

Still, whoever had killed Lester had thought they were. The killer also had to have known Lester was attempting to smuggle the recorder out of the White House. The motive couldn't be clearer. They just hadn't counted on Lester hiding the recorder so well. If the killer ever learned that Jimmie had the recordings in his possession now, they would come after him.

This was a most unwelcome realization.

The dots that had seemed rather random were beginning to connect. A web was forming, with Jimmie smack-dab in the middle of it. Regardless of the fact that Lester didn't have anything on Trump, he'd told people he had—and someone had killed him for it.

Jimmie thought back to the list of people who had had access to the White House roof: Christie, Lewandowski, Putin. Each had a motive to protect Trump. It had to be one of them. A political scandal was brewing, the likes of which nobody had seen since Watergate. He knew next to nothing about that scandal, of course, and hoped to keep it that way. In his high school civics class, they'd watched *All the President's Men*. He'd fallen asleep fifteen minutes into it and woke up during the end credits and was assured by a classmate he hadn't missed a damn thing.

But he wasn't going to fall asleep now. At least not before three o'clock (one of his three naptimes, back when he was a freelancer). He could smell something fishy, and it wasn't the tuna sandwich he'd forgotten about in his desk drawer.

He hid the recorder back in the ceiling; he'd figure out how to get rid of it later, if necessary.

This wasn't Jimmie Bernwood being paranoid.

This was Jimmie Bernwood being smart.

In order to investigate this thing, though, he was going to have to do something stupid: He was going to have to enlist the help of his ex-lover.

One of them, that was. He had many, just so you know.

More than he could count.

(Seven.)

Only one, however, worked in the White House.

CHAPTER THIRTY-ONE

★ ★ ★ ★

THE BIRDS AND THE BEES

Jimmie watched from the sidelines as the president fielded questions from the pool of reporters.

"So what if England was our friend? Think how boring it would be if the Yankees and Red Sox were friends. Snoozefest. People like a healthy rivalry. Though I wouldn't call England the Red Sox. Maybe more like the Twins."

That got a surprisingly large laugh from the press corps. Jimmie surveyed the journalists, all of whom were fenced inside a wire pen. He recognized a couple. Keith Olbermann, who was on his sixth time around with ESPN. Joe Buck, from Fox Sports. Vin Scully, the former Dodgers play-by-play announcer. In fact, more than half of the journalists appeared to be from the world of sports. This was, apparently, standard practice for days when the Donald took the podium. They didn't want questions from anyone who'd done too much research.

Jimmie smiled as a feeling of superiority swelled in his chest. Not because he was better than them, but because he was probably making twice what they were making. Maybe that was the same thing—it didn't matter. All that mattered was that amongst the fifty or so reporters of varying degrees of triviality was Cat Diaz, whose hand was held high.

Trump called on her.

"Mr. President, do you plan to respond to Prince Charles's latest comments?" Cat asked. She had her clear thick-rimmed glasses on today, the ones that did funny things to Jimmie.

"I assume you mean that clown's speech before Parliament, where he called me an embarrassment to swine," Trump said. "We're meeting to determine a really primo insult to send back across the pond."

"Could you give us a preview of some of the names being discussed?" Cat asked.

"That's classified, sorry," Trump said. "You gotta keep an eye on my Twitter feed. I will say this, though. He's a very ugly man—I mean, I've seen elephants with smaller ears. He's an ugly man who married way, way above his station in the looks department, married a total fox, and then he cheated on her. So the man's clearly an idiot. I would never have cheated on Lady Di. Never. And I cheat on everybody."

There was more laughter from the sports reporters as Trump ended the session and left the room.

Jimmie hopped into the press corps pen and waded through the sea of journalists, who were packing their notebooks away. He made a beeline for Cat. Come to think of it, though, he'd never seen a bee fly in a straight line. Usually they zigzagged around, looking for the right flower to bang.

Cat took one look at Jimmie and turned the other way.

She had no interest in being his flower.

Or maybe—just maybe—she was playing hard to get.

"Wait up," he said, reaching out for her. His hand landed on her shoulder. Immediately, he realized this was a poor decision on his part. She dropped her notebook and gripped his wrist with both hands. She gave his arm a twist, which he felt all the way up to his shoulder. He spun down to the ground and found himself pinned to the floor with his arm bent unnaturally back in a *kimura* lock.

"You've been working out," he said through the pain.

"You haven't been," she said.

That much was true. He wasn't going to turn the tables on her. None of the other journalists seemed to even take notice that she had him writhing in pain on the carpet. Working in the Trump White House, they'd probably seen violent outbursts before. Rumor was, on Wednesday nights, the Bush Room transformed into a fight club.

Jimmie had no choice but to say his safeword: "E. L. James."

CHAPTER THIRTY-TWO

★ ★ ★ ★

HELLO KITTY

Cat released Jimmie. While the press corps had pretty much cleared out except for a few stragglers, prying eyes and ears could be anywhere. In the potted plants. In the luxury umbrella stand. In Cat's phone.

"Can we talk?" he said. "Somewhere private."

"You cost me my job, you idiot," she said. "And just how drunk were you last night at the State Dinner?"

Her job? Following the Ted Cruz sex tape lawsuit, she'd been the one who'd fired *him*. He eyed the logo on her badge. "You're still with the *Daily Blabber*, though."

"I was demoted to the presidential beat," she said. "You think I enjoy being penned up in here with these losers?"

Michael Strahan gave her a little wave, and Cat fake-smiled back. When he passed, the warmth once again drained from Cat's face.

She said, "You want to talk, Jimmie? I've got about five minutes until I have to be on the South Lawn golf course for Trump's big foreign policy speech."

"I'm headed there too," Jimmie said, although this was the first he'd heard about it. He really needed to start reading the daily e-mail with the president's schedule.

He followed her through the winding maze of hallways that he assumed would become second nature to him. If he stayed at the White House long enough.

"What are you doing tonight?" Jimmie said, opening the door for her to the back lawn. Two dozen rows of chairs were quickly filling for the soon-to-be-historic speech. "Let me take you out to dinner. As an apology for all the trouble I caused you."

"There's not a restaurant in this city expensive enough to make up for all the trouble you've caused me," she said.

Likewise, he thought.

"Do you have your phone on you?" he asked.

"What's this really about?"

"Just answer the question."

"It's at my desk."

"Good," he said, lowering his voice. "Because I need to talk to you about Lester."

"Are you still angry about that? If I remember correctly, *you* were the one who proposed that we 'take a break.'"

"So that means you go sleeping around on me?"

"That's *exactly* what that means."

Okay, so maybe she had a point. Things had been moving kind of fast between them at the time. They'd gone from sleeping together to living together in under a month. That, coupled with working together, had spooked Jimmie. So, yeah, he'd suggested they take a break from each other. He thought he'd move back into his own apartment. Maybe go to a movie on a Friday night by himself. He hadn't expected to be replaced by Lester fucking Dorset.

Jimmie asked, "When's the last time you spoke to Lester?"

She ignored him and picked up her pace.

"He was working as Trump's ghostwriter," Jimmie said, jogging after her. "A job that I've been hired for, as of Monday."

"You're both idiots for working with that guy. He's a racist, a sexist—"

"That's just a bunch of talk. He seems okay in person."

Except for when he asked his Secret Service detail to shoot me, Jimmie thought. But he could see why Cat wouldn't like him: Her father was Mexican (one of the good ones, but still). That, plus the fact that she was a woman, meant she wasn't exactly Trump's target market.

"Well, have fun while it lasts," Cat said. "I hear Trump likes to fire people."

"Lester wasn't fired."

"So he quit," she said. "So what? We split up a while back. I don't keep tabs on him."

"You don't know, do you?"

"Know *what*?"

Jimmie lowered his voice: "He's dead."

Cat stopped abruptly, and Jimmie slammed into her.

"I'm sorry to be the one to tell you," he said.

Her bottom lip quivered. He shouldn't have sprung this on her here. There was a time and a place to tell your ex-girlfriend that her dickhead boyfriend was dead, and this wasn't it.

"I haven't spoken to him in months," Cat said. "June? Earlier, maybe. I don't know. We didn't see each other around the

West Wing too often—Corey keeps the press corps on a pretty tight leash to prevent anyone from leaking real news to us. I just . . . I can't believe it. I would have heard if something happened to him. Are you sure?"

Jimmie nodded.

"How did he die?" she asked.

He shook his head. "He last signed in to the White House on Independence Day. I have reason to believe that was also the day he died. I can't say more now . . . but could you just meet me tonight? Or even after this event. Maybe we could grab a drink."

She was quiet for a long time.

Finally, she said, "Did they give you his old office? He didn't . . . leave anything behind, did he?"

"Like . . ."

"Like, duh, *nudes*," she said.

"You let him take nude pictures of you?"

"We got one of those instant cameras and took some glamour shots in the vice president's office. Biden left behind his beanbag chair, where we—" She paused. "You know what, let's just meet Friday. I need a few days to process this. It's just . . . I can't believe it."

"Of course," he said.

"Oh, and another thing, before you even ask," she said. "I'm not going to sleep with you."

"That's good, because I wasn't going to ask," he said.

Cat disappeared into a row toward the back, and Jimmie took a seat up front.

She suspected he wanted to sleep with her. Ha! Part of him did—*that* part—but he had another, more pressing motive, one that he would spring on her over dinner. He needed her help.

Jimmie had three solid suspects for Lester's murder. If he could establish a prior relationship between Lester and one of them, he would save some time. That would help narrow his investigation—and possibly keep him alive, if he could sort out friends from foes inside La Casa Blanca.

Figuring out the *whodunit* was only step one. For step two, he needed a platform. With the FCC's ruling on net neutrality limiting the reach of small blogs, he couldn't just publish this story—no matter how big—by himself online and expect traction. The *Cigar Aficionado* editor had stopped returning his e-mails. With his name still blackballed across the industry, selling an exclusive to the *Daily Blabber* was his only hope. And this time, he wouldn't get slapped with a lawsuit. He'd get slapped with a Pulitzer. Then, and only then, would he ask to sleep with her. If she said yes, he might actually do it, too.

CHAPTER THIRTY-THREE

★ ★ ★ ★

PRINCE OF WHALES

"**P**ee-wee Paul Ryan says the lawmaking process in this country is broken, and for once I agree with him," Trump said. "Maybe we should do things a little more like our good friend Russia. What is it you do over there, Vlad? You write it down and hand it to a bird, right?"

Putin, seated beside the president, nodded. "Is owl."

"That's right," Trump continued. "You write the law down—say, no more abortions after the fourth trimester—hand it to the owl, and send the owl out into a snowstorm. If it stops snowing within twenty-four hours, the bill becomes law. If not, you just try again, I guess?"

"We have many owl," Putin said with a tight-lipped smile.

The president was just over ten minutes into his remarks, but already Jimmie's mind was wandering. He looked down at his open notebook. He hadn't taken a single note so far during the event, unless you counted the sketch of the first family's wiener dog. It had shown up, humped the leg of a Secret Service agent for three minutes, and then chased off after a squirrel into the Rose Garden. Opulence was probably humping the poor squirrel right now.

"I'm issuing all these executive orders, but there's no funding for any of them. They'd just sit there if I didn't find creative ways to fund them. Whoever thought about opening a Chase business card for the United States before? I was the first to do it. We're getting a very, very good rate, too. Plus Amazon rewards!

"Unfortunately," Trump continued, "there's this little document called the *Constitution*—"

A chorus of boos momentarily drowned Trump out.

"Settle down, settle down," he said, raising his voice. "The Founding Fathers can't hear you—they're dead! What do they care if the entire legislative branch is a joke?

"The pressure's on Congress now. I shouldn't have to go begging to them every time I want a few billion bucks or want to declare war on a bunch of tea-drinking pansies. If they don't give me the authority I want, maybe I'll just give it to myself. What do you think?"

Cheers from the audience. Jimmie glanced around to see who among the press corps was cheering—turned out, nobody. It appeared Trump had filled in the empty seats with ringers outfitted in Trump gear. One woman three rows behind Jimmie was wearing a shirt with a cartoon drawing of Prince Charles and several rather robust women, with the caption "PRINCE OF WHALES."

"The new process—and this could change—is that I'll write the bills myself and sign them. Then I'll hand them to my bald eagle courier, who will fly them to Massachusetts, where a Mayflower descendent will seal them into law by chiseling them into the Plymouth Rock. If that doesn't work out for whatever reason, we can always—"

"BEAR!"

Jimmie craned his neck around to see who'd interrupted the president. People were standing, row by row, and exiting in a panic. They were being split down the middle, like a parting sea. All hell was breaking loose in slow motion.

"Bear?" Trump said. "No, we're going to use an *eagle*—"

Jimmie heard the great beast before he saw it. The creature's deep, bass growl rumbled across the green, like thunder across the Midwest plains of Jimmie's youth. The hairs on the back of his neck stood at attention, even as he was frozen in place.

"What in the hell is going on out there? I'm not finished!" Trump yelled into the microphone. "I'm not finished!"

Trump's demand fell on deaf ears. People were fleeing the seating gallery haphazardly, tipping their folding chairs over. Cat ran past Jimmie on her way back into the White House, where everyone seemed to be headed for cover.

That's when Jimmie finally saw the animal cutting its way through the middle of the crowd.

It was no bear.

It was a giant panda.

Which was technically a bear, Jimmie supposed.

He also recognized this one: Mei Xiang, the adult female from the National Zoo. Not only had she survived Trump and Putin's hunt, but she'd escaped! Maybe they'd released the animals from their cages and made the hunt a little more sporting than Jimmie had first thought.

The panda batted chairs to the left and to the right with its massive tree-trunk arms, roaring all the while. Its dark eyes blended into the black patches of fur that encircled them, but Jimmie was sure he could see more than a flicker of rage in them. This creature was out for blood. This creature was out for *revenge*.

CHAPTER THIRTY-FOUR

★ ★ ★ ★

MEI XIANG'S REVENGE

When the panda was fifteen yards away, Jimmie's fight-or-flight instinct finally kicked in. He crouched low and dashed to the edge of the seated area just as a chair flew over his head. Thankfully for Jimmie, the panda was of a single mind. It may not have been moving fast, but there was a deliberateness to its path of destruction. The panda was headed straight for the president of the United States and his entourage.

Although Trump had finally given up on his speech, he refused to yield the podium. "I'm not letting some Chinese push me around!" he shouted.

A phalanx of Secret Service agents formed a semicircle around the president, weapons drawn. They were decked out in black suits that had to be hot as hell on a day like this under the sun. They were probably a bit tougher than Jimmie and not likely to complain like he would about such things. That was why they were guarding the president and Jimmie was watching helplessly from the literal sidelines.

They didn't fire at the panda. There were too many civilians behind the creature, standing around with their phones raised. Like Jimmie, they'd seen that the interloper wasn't just randomly attacking people. It was heading straight for a single target. So out came their phones to Periscope and YouTube and SnatchCatch it to the world.

Vladimir Putin emerged from the shield of Secret Service agents with a shotgun. Where he'd picked up a shotgun was anyone's guess, but he had one.

"Stand down, Americans," Putin hissed. "This is between me and woman bear."

Upon seeing Putin's receding hairline, the giant panda charged forward at full speed. Jimmie had only seen pandas sitting around in zoos, napping and occasionally eating shoots and leaves. He'd never seen a panda drop to all fours and go from zero to sixty in two seconds.

Before Putin could raise the barrel of the shotgun, the panda hit him like a semi plowing into a Smart electric car.

The shotgun went flying as Putin was slammed into the ground. The giant panda rolled him over onto his stomach to assume a more dominant position. Then the beast pawed at his back, ripping Putin's shirt clean off. The sow raked its massive claws across the Russian's exposed flesh, drawing blood.

The Secret Service agents exchanged glances with each other, unsure whether to intervene.

Trump held up a hand, as if to say, *Let the fight go on.*

The panda put one paw on the back of Putin's skull and pressed down with all its weight. A great cry of anguish issued forth from beneath the beast. Jimmie flinched. The Russian president was being crushed to death live on social media. This was certainly a first in the digital realm.

Putin struggled to get out from under the panda, but it was useless. The sow had to weigh at least two tons. That was a lot of shoots and leaves.

After another minute, Putin's arms and legs stopped twitching. The panda stood on its hind legs and roared in victory.

Jimmie saw that Putin still had some fight left in him, however. The Russian president inched his hand down the side of his leg, where he found a six-inch bowie knife hidden underneath his dress pants.

The panda didn't look down until it was too late. Putin rolled over onto his back (or what was left of it) and hopped to a standing position. It was a feat of athletic prowess that Jimmie had only seen before on the WWE. The panda cocked its head in confusion at the shirtless, bloodied man attempting to stand toe-to-toe with it. Despite Putin's impressive stature, the panda towered several feet over him.

Before the panda could react, the Russian president ran the knife up through the bear's ribs and straight into its heart.

The panda staggered backward on its hind legs, with the handle of the knife sticking out of its chest. It flailed its arms about and howled in pain. It took a few more ragged breaths before stumbling forward, right on top of the man who had struck it down. Two tons of dead weight fell on Putin, crumpling him like he was an empty can of Trump Cola.

✷ ✷ ✷ ✷

Excerpt From the Trump/Dorset Sessions

July 1, 2018, 7:49 AM

DORSET: The race for the White House was a wild one. On the Republican side, you battled it out with more than a dozen other serious contenders—

TRUMP: I would hardly call them "serious." There was only ever one serious candidate for the Republican nomination. His name was Donald J. Trump.

DORSET: You certainly garnered the majority of votes. Still, Ted Cruz, the junior senator from Texas, gave you a run for your money late in the campaign.

TRUMP: Lying Ted Cruz? Don't get me started on that guy. We all saw what happened to him in the end. Terribly sad. I knew he was a liar. I take no pleasure in being right about him, you know. I wish he'd been caught sooner, but he's behind bars now.

DORSET: I'd like to ask you about that. After you were sworn in, one of your first actions was to have the FBI reopen the Zodiac Killer case. Within a matter of weeks, they had arrested a suspect in the series of grisly killings that took place in California during the late sixties and early seventies: Ted Cruz.

TRUMP: Brilliant work by the FBI.

DORSET: The Zodiac Killer's first confirmed murder, a double homicide in Solano County, was in December of 1968. Ted Cruz was born in Calgary in December of 1970.

TRUMP: Being born in Canada doesn't preclude someone from being a serial killer. It does preclude them from being president of the United States of America, but that's another story entirely.

DORSET: I'm asking if it makes any sense that he's the Zodiac Killer, given that all five of the murders law enforcement attributed to him occurred before he was even born.

TRUMP: Ask the jury. I wasn't in the courtroom. I didn't see the evidence.

DORSET: You really believe a jury could legitimately convict somebody for murders that couldn't be committed without a time machine?

TRUMP: I have faith in our justice system. Answer me this: Since Lying Ted Cruz has been locked up, has there been another Zodiac Killer murder? No, there hasn't. I rest my case.

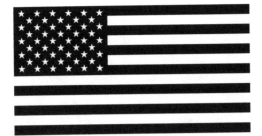

Thursday, August 30, 2018

CHAPTER THIRTY-FIVE

★ ★ ★ ★

THURSDAY,
DON'T EVEN START

Thursday was declared a day of national mourning for President Putin. Trump excused all White House employees for the day so everyone could honor the late Russian president's memory in their own way.

As Putin's body was flown home to Russia, Jimmie hit up the Leonardo DiCaprio triple feature at the nearby megaplex. Putin had once described the actor as a *muzhik*. A "real man." It was only fitting that both Putin and DiCaprio had gone out fighting bears—Putin at the White House and DiCaprio while filming *The Revenant 2*'s impressive live-grizzly attack scene (shot in one take, for which DiCaprio picked up a much-deserved posthumous Oscar).

It was while watching DiCaprio get torn apart by the pack of thirty-two hungry grizzlies that Jimmie finally concluded there was no way Putin could have had anything to do with Lester Dorset's death. The Russian president had gone down fighting a two-ton panda. Putin was a real man. It was utterly inconceivable that he would murder a reporter by pushing him from a roof in the middle of the night. That wasn't the way of the *muzhik*. Lester Dorset's killer was still out there. One suspect down . . . two to go.

★ ★ ★ ★

Excerpt From the Trump/Dorset Sessions

June 25, 2018, 8:16 AM

DORSET: You had some strong words for Jeb! Bush during the primaries.

TRUMP: He's a wimp. He has weak, limp wrists. A tiny voice. Low energy. He might be suffering from a medical condition. Have you heard of this? "Low T"?

DORSET: Low testosterone levels. Some doctors say "low T" is exaggerated as a medical condition—that it's natural for men's testosterone levels to drop as we age.

TRUMP: You know who doesn't suffer from low testosterone levels? Me, that's who. My doctor said my levels were off the charts. Literally so high they would need to recalibrate the testing equipment.

DORSET: That sounds potentially dangerous.

TRUMP: I should find a way to take my excess and bottle it. I could charge a fortune for it. You'd buy it.

DORSET: Uh . . . I don't know that—

TRUMP: You'd buy it. Come on. Besides, who would you rather have in the White House? Somebody with too much testosterone or a wimp like Jeb! with too little?

DORSET: I'm not sure if testosterone levels equate to sound governance. We'd have to check to see if any studies have been done.

TRUMP: You don't need a study to tell you that it takes "high T" to do what I do. It takes a pair of big balls to be commander in chief. When Jeb!'s finally drop, he's welcome to come out of whatever Florida swamp hole he's been hiding in and come at me like a man. I will fight him any day of the week. Except on Sunday. Sundays are reserved for golf and *Game of Thrones*.

DORSET: You've been almost as critical of Jeb!'s brother, George W. Bush, as you were of Obama.

TRUMP: The Iraq War was a disaster. How many trillions of dollars did we sink into that waste of time? If we'd gotten some oil out of it, it might have been worth it. How hard is that? Throw some empty jugs in the Humvee. He made the same mistake his father made with Kuwait. To quote *The Art of War*, "Never get into a land war in Asia."

DORSET: You've been very vocal about the need to "bomb the shit out of ISIS." The United States' use of unmanned drones in the Middle East has increased dramatically under your leadership.

TRUMP: We're bombing the shit out of them—their training camps, their weapons stockpiles, and so forth. All from the air with our little toy planes. Since I took office, not one American life has been lost overseas.

DORSET: While that's made you wildly popular with the American people, it's brought condemnation from some quarters. Drone warfare is still warfare. The *Guardian*'s George Monbiot has said the US is "fighting a coward's war."

TRUMP: The *Guardian*? How typical. Of course the Brits would call us names—they're still nursing their wounds from when we ran them out of town in seventeen-whatever. They're a nation of cowards, I tell you. They make France look like goddamn Sparta.

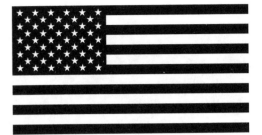

Friday, August 31, 2018

CHAPTER THIRTY-SIX

★ ★ ★ ★

A LITTLE DITTY

After an exhausting day of totally boring meetings, Jimmie found himself with an hour to kill until he was supposed to meet Cat for dinner. Most of the staffers had left early for the day to get a head start on Labor Day weekend. As good a time as any to dispose of Lester's recorder.

He removed it from its hiding spot. The worthless "game-changing" interviews on it had already gotten two men killed. Jimmie had no desire to be the third. And yet . . . he couldn't quite bring himself to just ditch it. It might come in handy—as evidence for the emerging story. Right now, there was precious little to hold onto. He didn't know where Lester was buried, and Connor Brent was fish food.

There was a knock at the door. He panicked, stashed the recorder in his desk, and then answered the door.

"You're not answering your phone," Chris Christie said, bursting in like Meat Loaf on a motorcycle.

It wasn't a question. It was an accusation.

"The battery must be dead," Jimmie said, pulling the door shut.

"Don't lie to me," Christie said, muscling his way past Jimmie. He sniffed the air. "I'm from Jersey. I can smell a lie from a mile away."

"You know, Emma's phone died Monday morning. Maybe we need new phones. Are we eligible for upgrades?"

"Not sure why somebody would lie about their battery being dead?" Chris Christie paced the length of the room (which wasn't more than five paces) and spun on his heel. "Let me tell you a little story about a couple of kids named Jack and Diane. They grew up together in the American heartland. One of 'em thought he was gonna be a football star someday. The other was just along for the ride in the back of her boyfriend's car. I think you can see where I'm going with this."

"Is this a John Cougar Mellencamp song?"

"Maybe," Christie said. "But just because Johnny Cougar sang about it, doesn't mean it didn't happen. What I'm trying to say is that Jack wanted to run off to the city, but Diane wasn't having none of that. But Jack . . . well, Jack was restless. He left one day for LA to be the next James Deen. Became one of them porno stars out there. Forgot all about playing football, which I suppose I would too."

"I suppose."

"Damn right you suppose," Christie said. "But he eventually turns to drugs. Gets in a bad way. Can't perform no more. Life goes on, though, a long time after the thrill of living is gone. He's depressed, and he thinks about Diane. Sweet Diane. By this point, he's gone balls deep in hundreds of girls, but she's still the only one he's ever loved. He texts her, and she doesn't answer."

"Because her phone is dead."

"Except that it wasn't. She'd seen his text but ignored him. She wasn't sure if she wanted to get all mixed up with Jack again. But that text . . . the more she thought about it, the more she thought about leaving her husband and kids behind. You see, for her, life had gone on too. The thrill wasn't there either. Finally, she texted him back: 'Sorry, my phone died. Didn't see your text.' But it was too late. Jack was dead. He'd taken an overdose of Viagra. His wiener exploded."

"That's terrible," Jimmie said. "And this really happened?"

"I have no idea. I'm just telling you why someone would lie about their battery being dead. That's just one reason. I could probably think of . . . a few more. Another kid named Tommy, used to work down on the docks. His gal Gina's working at the diner all day. They're both down on their luck, just trying to hold on to what they GOT!"

Christie slammed a large paw down on the desk, which rattled the fillings in Jimmie's back teeth. The drawer slid open, and Christie peered over the desk into it. "Do you mind . . . ?"

"Go ahead," Jimmie said as Christie picked his phone up. He thought he saw Christie's eyes linger on the recorder, but maybe that was Jimmie's paranoia.

Christie held down the power button. Jimmie's screen saver flashed on the phone.

"Cute girls," Christie said. "These your kids?"

Christie'd been at every Trump rally to date, right behind the president . . . and he didn't know who was on Jimmie's screen saver?

"Those are the USA Freedom Girls for America," Jimmie said. "They're all legal. In some states."

Christie snorted. "Looks like your battery is fine, wouldn't you say—"

The screen went black.

Christie thrust the dead phone into Jimmie's hands. "Keep it charged from now on, okay? Emma was trying to reach you for the past forty-five minutes. Thought maybe you'd gone home, but I said I'd check up on you. And here you are."

"Here I am," Jimmie said. "Do you know what she wanted?"

"A half hour opened up in the president's schedule. He wants to talk to you."

Jimmie plugged his phone into his charger. When he turned around, Christie was still blocking the door.

"One more thing," Christie said, reaching into his suit jacket . . .

CHAPTER THIRTY-SEVEN

★ ★ ★ ★

HAVE YOU HEARD THE GOOD WORD?

Christie's hand emerged with a burgundy, leather-bound Bible. He hadn't pegged Christie as a Bible-thumper, but stranger things had happened. Here he was, trying to recruit Jimmie over to the side of the angels. Good luck with that.

"Thanks, but I already have a Bible I don't read," Jimmie said.

"I know—you left it behind at the Royal Linoleum," Christie said.

"I left it behind . . . ?" Jimmie's voice trailed off as it hit him: This was the Gideon Bible from his bedside table. The one he'd marked up with Morris code.

This isn't happening, he thought. *This can't be happening.*

Jimmie was beginning to have a hard time distinguishing between his imagination and reality. Maybe he'd suffocated in that tunnel underneath the wall. His comatose body could be laid out in some Mexican hospital right now while all of this was happening in his head. One long dream from which he might never wake up.

You know you're in desperate straits when the best-case scenario is that you're in a permanent coma.

145

Christie said, "I did a little security sweep, to make sure you hadn't left any sensitive material behind. Thought at first this was placed there by the hotel, but then I saw the inscription on the inside." Christie's eyes met his. "The inscription from your mother."

"My mother?"

"Her message seemed to be . . . of a personal nature. A *very* personal nature," Christie said, handing the Bible over. "It's fortunate I discovered it, wouldn't you say?"

Jimmie cracked the Bible and peeked at the chicken-scratches he'd left in it. Chris Christie wasn't so stupid as to believe this was a message from Jimmie's mother . . . unless his mother was a Socialist Justice Warrior.

The book trembled in Jimmie's hands. The fact that Jimmie wasn't in some Guantanamo Bay dungeon right now was significant. The fact that Christie was covering for him was even more so. While Christie might have been dangerous, he hadn't killed Lester—because if he had, he would have killed Jimmie right now and made off with the recorder.

"You've got three minutes to get upstairs to the Oval Office," Christie said, glancing at his watch. "Mr. Trump can't stand tardiness. You want to hold on to what *you* got, I suggest you get a move on it, Jimmie-boy."

CHAPTER THIRTY-EIGHT

★ ★ ★ ★

LAST MAN STANDING

Jimmie took the stairs two at a time and burst into the Reagan Library. His heart was pounding like he'd just hiked to the tip of the Washington Monument. His mind was spinning from what had just happened with Christie. If the White House janitor was indeed sympathetic to the Bernie bros, he couldn't have had anything to do with Lester's death. That left one suspect on Jimmie's list: Corey Lewandowski.

Jimmie went out of his way to avoid passing Lewandowski's office on his way to meet the president. He wasn't taking a chance. The Secret Service agents who were usually stationed every twenty yards had taken off for the weekend. He picked up his speed, even as he felt the beginnings of a cramp in his right side.

Emma's door was open. She wasn't at her desk—probably gone home for the day like everyone else. Now that it was past five on Friday, the government was all but shut down for the holiday weekend. Jimmie raced through her office, which adjoined the Oval Office.

He glanced at the clock on her wall and saw that he'd made it—miraculously, he'd made it with seconds to spare. The doors to the Oval Office were open a crack. He threw open the double doors and was immediately tackled to the ground.

CHAPTER THIRTY-NINE

✫ ✫ ✫ ✫

WHAT'S OUR VECTOR, VICTOR?

For the second time in one week, Jimmie found himself pinned to the floor of the White House. The golden shag in the Oval Office was loads nicer than the worn, industrial carpet in the press corps pen.

Still, that didn't make the experience any more pleasant. Corey Lewandowski had hit him squarely in the ribs with a football tackle. He'd heard about getting the wind knocked out of you but had never truly appreciated just how accurate of a description it was until his lungs went flat inside his chest.

His brain felt fuzzy. He was flat on his stomach on the floor, so how was he face-to-face with the Donald? He inhaled a shaky breath, and his surroundings swam into focus: He was lying on a picture of the Donald—shirtless, holding an olive branch in one hand and a bunch of arrows in the other—woven into the carpet on the Oval Office floor.

He tried to roll over, but Lewandowski had a foot on Jimmie's back.

"I had an appointment," Jimmie said.

"Shut up or you're going to have an appointment with my fist," Lewandowski said.

It sounded to Jimmie like the press secretary was ready to kill him here—no waiting until darkness and throwing him off the roof. Out of the corner of one eye, Jimmie could see Trump peeking his head out over the desk. Just the hedgehog-like hair and a pair of orange-rimmed, beady eyes were visible.

"Let him up," Trump said, rising to his feet.

Lewandowski stared at the president. "Surely you must be joking."

"Don't call me Shirley," Trump said.

"Sir?"

"It's from *Airplane!*," Trump said.

"Roger, Roger," Jimmie squeaked out.

Lewandowski pressed his foot harder into Jimmie's back. "Didn't I tell you to keep quiet?"

"Let him up and hit the golden showers," Trump said. "Give us a little private time."

Gradually, the pressure on Jimmie's back decreased as the press secretary lifted his foot as slowly as humanly possible. Jimmie thought he might give him a kick on the way out, but Lewandowski simply slammed the doors behind him.

Jimmie rolled over and again was face-to-face with Donald Trump. This time, in the form of the painting on the Oval Office ceiling—a version of Michelangelo's *The Creation of Adam*, except Adam's face had been replaced by Trump's.

And so had God's.

Jimmie pulled himself to his feet and located the one real Trump in the room.

Jimmie was alone with the president.

The president of the United States of America.

The man who had made America great again.

"I would apologize for that, but you really should knock before entering," Trump said, sitting down and inviting Jimmie to do the same. The president leaned back in his great leather chair and kicked his feet up onto the desk. A flattened hundred-dollar bill was stuck to the bottom of one of Trump's shoes by a yellowish splotch of gum.

"The door was cracked open," Jimmie said, sitting across from Trump. "But lesson learned. I thought there'd be Secret Service around, though?"

Trump shrugged. "You all settled into your office?"

"Getting there. Need to put up some posters and make it feel like home."

"I need to do that around here. All I've got up now are these fancy works of art. Like that Rembrandt over there," Trump said, pointing out the *Mona Lisa*. Probably the original. "A little stuffy, if you ask me. I can't stand modern art, but some of this old crap is as boring as a national security briefing. Like, would it kill you to put a rack on that gal?"

"I'm not an art man myself."

Trump sighed. "Least it's better than the tacky shit in the vice president's office. A wife like that and all the photos are of Gronkowski. Jumping Jesus on a pogo stick.

"You know," Trump continued, "I like you. I've always liked your work. Your *Daily Blabber* column was one of the few sites I read. Just a shame what happened. You should have gotten a presidential Medal of Honor for what you did for the country."

"I'll settle for a Purple Heart," Jimmie said, rubbing his cracked ribs.

"I'll see what I can do," Trump said. "I trust the Watergate is meeting your expectations? It's a world-class property. One of my favorites."

"I appreciate you setting me up there—it's like night and day compared to the last place I stayed. No one's broken into my room, at least."

"You had a break-in at the Royal Linoleum?" Trump pulled his feet off the desk and invited Jimmie to follow him. "C'mon. Let's get some exercise."

As they exited the Oval Office, they passed a Secret Service agent. "Humble is on the move," the agent said, speaking into his wrist. "Humble is on the move."

CHAPTER FORTY

★ ★ ★ ★

HUMBLE IS ON THE MOVE

"You're not the first person to do this job," Trump said as they strolled down the hall. A pair of Secret Service agents trailed them.

Jimmie considered feigning ignorance but decided to roll the dice. There was no sense playing stupid around the man who was the master at playing stupid.

"Lester Dorset," Jimmie said. "We weren't friends or anything, but I knew him."

"I had a feeling you would find out about him," Trump said. "You're a good reporter—you can sniff stuff out. I'm a little concerned you may have the wrong idea about what happened to Lester."

"I don't have any idea, actually."

"That's good," Trump said. "You know, the *New York Times* was never nice to me. My hometown paper, and they would say the most awful things about me! I should have bought them. I could have, you know. I had the money."

"We're often hardest on those closest to us. In my experience."

Trump snorted. "Well, nobody was harder on me at that paper than Lester Dorset. One time, in the nineties, he wrote something personal about me—something about my first

152

wife and the alimony. I called him up and chewed him a new asshole."

"I'm sure he deserved it."

"You know what he did, though? He stopped writing about me for six months. That was his punishment."

Jimmie followed Trump up the Grand Staircase.

"I learned then that I'd rather have someone write something bad about me than write nothing at all," Trump said. "If it's painful, the hurt goes away in a day or two. But if there's nothing there . . . just some void . . . the ache just grows and grows. I never liked Lester Dorset, but I respected him. That's why I hired him when I had the chance."

The Secret Service had stopped trailing them. Jimmie looked over his shoulder with worry. Trump must have seen the look on his face, because he said, "The Secret Service doesn't come up to the second and third floors. They think the family quarters are haunted."

"Are they?"

"I don't believe in ghosts," Trump said.

That didn't necessarily answer the question, but Jimmie let it slide.

They entered the Lincoln Bedroom. "Are you carrying a phone? Anything electronic?" Trump asked. "Take it out and leave it on the dresser before we go outside."

Jimmie's phone was in the subbasement charging, but he'd brought the recorder with him—he didn't trust Christie, not entirely. If Trump recognized it as Lester's, he'd be screwed.

Jimmie set the recorder down. He watched Trump for a reaction. There was no sign of recognition on the president's face. All audio recorders probably looked the same to him.

"One of the many upgrades I added around here," Trump said, opening a great pair of double doors. "Private patios for the family quarters."

He ushered Jimmie onto a deck overlooking the backyard—the same deck where he'd seen the first lady in her towel. Jimmie shielded his eyes from the glare of the gold-plated Washington Monument.

Trump put a hand on the railing and pointed up. Jimmie craned his neck to look at the curved overhead ceiling. "He was up there, on top of the roof," Trump said. "There are multiple snipers stationed up there at all times. But they're focused on external threats to the White House: someone jumping the gate or streaking across the lawn. Nobody saw Lester up there until he was at the edge of the roof. By then, it was too late. He jumped."

Trump whistled while tracing the man's path off the roof and down into the garden of flowers below. The Rose Garden.

"It was just after ten, I believe," Trump said, now peering over the railing and into the flower bed below. "Very, very dark. There was a Secret Service agent stationed just a few yards from the Rose Garden. He thought we were under attack, by ninjas jumping off the roof or some shit. I mean, who wouldn't think that?"

"Seems reasonable," Jimmie said.

"He ordered Lester to stay on the ground. It was a goddamn miracle, but Lester wasn't dead. He'd survived the fall and was laying there with a broken leg. Two broken arms. Broken everything. But he was still alive." Trump paused. "Until he tried to stand, and the Secret Service fellow shot him six times, square in the chest. It would have been a great, great embarrassment to the Secret Service," Trump said. "For one thing—shooting an unarmed man. I mean, thank God he was white, right?"

Jimmie didn't say anything.

"Since it happened so late, and in almost total darkness, we swept it under the rug. More or less. Not just because it would embarrass the Secret Service, but because it would embarrass Lester. His wife and children didn't need to know that their father had taken his own life—the coward's way out. It was better for them to think he'd gone hiking. Which, come to think of it, is such a cowardly thing to do too. It's like going hunting without carrying a gun."

"Do you know why he did it?"

"No note," Trump said. "Not even a Snapchat. He wasn't struggling financially, from what my people could tell—we would have helped him out if we'd known about any difficulties. He was doing great work. Fantastic work. We'd spent hours talking in the Oval Office, which is all lost now, I suppose."

The president's usual hyperbole had temporarily gone dormant.

"Afterward, my advisors and I spent hours watching and listening to tapes of him, looking for clues," Trump said. "There are eyes and ears everywhere, Jimmie. Even the bathrooms."

Jimmie already had a shy enough bladder as it was— he didn't know how he was ever going to use the restroom at the White House again. Thank God there was a Starbucks across the street.

"Unfortunately, there's only so much time one man has," Trump said. "When you're the leader of the free world, you don't have the time to do everything yourself. What good are a hundred different surveillance tapes if you don't have time to watch them? You have to outsource tasks to people you trust. People who don't need to check in every fifteen minutes for your stamp of approval. I give my staff a lot of leeway. It's the same thing I tell my pilot: Fly the plane. As long as it takes off and lands, I've got bigger things to deal with."

Jimmie nodded.

"The trouble is," Trump continued, "when people see you're distracted or your attention is elsewhere, they take that as a sign that it's okay to slack off. Or worse: They think they can take advantage of you. Same thing happened with my casinos in Atlantic City. Unless I was there, on-site, things just went to hell. And Atlantic City was also just kind of like hell, so I preferred to spend as little time as possible there. If you had the choice between a penthouse overlooking Central Park and a dump on a boardwalk in Jersey, which would you choose?"

"I—"

"Exactly," Trump cut in. "You'd take Manhattan. Anyone would. God, I wish I were back in New York."

"It's a beautiful city," Jimmie said. It had been his home, too, for nearly a decade.

"Some days, I think of just taking off in my chopper and heading back to Trump Tower. Leave Washington and all these dirty politicians behind. But I would never do that. I made a promise to the American people, and I'm not leaving until I'm finished with that promise. We're winning. By the time I'm done with this country, they're going to be so tired of winning, they'll elect some loser to take my place. Paul Ryan, or some schmuck who will do his best to cock up everything I'll have accomplished."

"Seems to be how the political cycle works."

"It's dumb—it's a cycle of ignorance. The people think they know what they want, but when you give it to them, they change their minds. Democracy is a broken system. If you want to get anything done, you need to lead from the top down, not the bottom up. Look at the Empire."

"The Ottoman Empire?"

"The *Empire* Empire. *Star Wars*. Darth Vader. Say what you will about his parental skills, but that guy knew how to get shit done. He built not one but two Death Stars. You know how many of his citizens he put to work on those projects? The scale is unimaginable. A small group of agitators—the Rebels—destroyed everything he'd worked for." Trump lowered his voice. "We have a Rebel Alliance in this country, plotting against me as we speak. They call themselves 'Socialist Justice Warriors.' We haven't had a Kardashian attack on US soil during my presidency, and suddenly I've got these domestic terrorists to deal with? Give me a break!"

As far as Jimmie was aware, there hadn't *ever* been a Kardashian attack on US soil—or internationally, for that matter. While Trump may have been misguided there, he was correct about the Rebel Alliance. One for two wasn't bad.

"Not only that," Trump continued, "but we have a leak in the White House."

CHAPTER FORTY-ONE

★ ★ ★ ★

LET'S GO CUBBIES

The blood in Jimmie's veins went ice-cold. Did Trump suspect that he was the leak? Sure, he'd met with a Socialist Justice Warrior in Clinton Plaza. Had Christie showed Trump the Gideon Bible? Even though he'd rejected the offer, he hadn't reported the meeting to law enforcement. That probably made him as good as guilty in Trump's eyes.

"We can speak freely out here," Trump said, mistaking the reason for his silence. "There are white-noise generators at both ends of the veranda, which we bought from Hillary's staff at a yard sale. Even the Secret Service can't hear us from the Rose Garden below."

Jimmie swallowed hard. "You said there was a plot against the White House?"

"Homeland Security picks up chatter from time to time. Kardashians, mostly. We hear things on social media, on texts. We read e-mails. But these SJWs are smart. They know how we operate. They don't communicate online. They use paper and pens; they use landlines. They're invisible to us."

"I hope I'm not out of line here . . . but, outside of a few protestors at rallies, are you sure they exist?"

"We have surveillance photos of a meeting of the agitators," Trump said. "We identified one of the rally leaders and tortured the hell out of him. He sings for some musical group named the Pearl Jams."

"I'm familiar with them," Jimmie said.

Trump raised an eyebrow.

"Their music, I mean."

"He gave us the name of who we assume is the leader of the rebel alliance," Trump said. "Jeremy."

"Do you know anything else about these . . . agitators?"

"They wear blue caps."

"That should make them easy to find, then," Jimmie said. "The obvious problem being that lots of *other* people wear blue caps. Like Chicago Cubs fans, for instance. Are you sure Eddie Vedder, a noted Chicago fan, wasn't simply wearing a Cubs cap?"

"You might be on to something there," Trump said. "We did pick him up at Wrigley Stadium. I might have to put in a call to Guantanamo." Trump rested his proportionally small hands on the railing and sighed. "You know, I wasn't too sure about you at first. You refuse to stay in the finest, most sumptuous hotel. You throw up on me. You're a different cat, Jimmie."

"Thank you?"

"When I said I handpicked you, I wasn't lying," Trump said. "Or I was, a little. Because although you're my new ghostwriter, there's another job that I wanted you for. I want you to help me find the leak in this administration. Be my plumber."

"Emma didn't mention anything about this."

"This is between me and you. You're one of the dirtiest players in the game. I had to get a feel for you before springing this on you, though."

"Emma doesn't know. What about Christie or Lewandowski?"

"This is between you and me and the man upstairs," Trump said. "Baby Jesus."

"I've never really done anything like this before," Jimmie said. Not only that, but Jimmie wasn't sure if he was *up* for this sort of political espionage. He didn't know if he could continue to hear the word "leak" without giggling.

"It's easy. When you find the leak, you tell me. No one else. I'll take care of it myself. Because, as you know, it's the only way to ensure something gets done properly. No offense."

"None taken," Jimmie said.

"It should go without saying that nothing less than the future of our great country is at stake here," Trump said. "If England continues taunting us and the shit goes down, we need to have all our dicks in a row. Enemies outside our country could conspire with those within our borders. That's why we need to clamp down on these PC clowns. I need to know now: Are you my guy?"

Jimmie was about to dive further into the web of political intrigue that already had a body count several times that of the Watergate and Lewinsky scandals combined. For the record, nobody had died in either of those scandals, but both had brought presidents to their knees. While Jimmie still didn't know the full extent of what was happening inside the Trump White House, it was bound to trump those so-called scandals. The Pulitzer would be his. And then Cat would see just what she was missing out on. If she was lucky, he might even take her back.

Jimmie Bernwood, with two fingers crossed behind his back, shook Trump's hand. "I'm your guy," he said.

Trump nodded. There was a long, awkward pause.

"Any plans for the three-day weekend?" Jimmie asked, trying to make casual conversation. Jimmie was terrible at casual conversation. Then again, he was terrible at formal conversation too.

"Mar-a-Lago," Trump said. "A little golf, a little cookout. And you?"

"Nothing much . . ." Jimmie slapped himself on the forehead. How could he have been so stupid? "Do you know what time it is?"

Trump looked at his Rolex. "Ten 'til six. You have somewhere to be?"

"Meeting an ex-girlfriend for dinner. Do you need me much longer, or . . . ?"

Trump waved him on. "Can I also give you some advice, though? When you're out at dinner, head into the men's room and crank one out. That way, you're less likely to be tempted to fall back into old habits. Take it from me: Ex-sex is one of the worst decisions you can make. Think with your big head, not your little head."

CHAPTER FORTY-TWO

★ ★ ★ ★

THE NATIONAL OUTLET MALL

After Jimmie doubled back downstairs to grab his charged phone, it was 6:08. He shot Cat a quick text letting her know he'd be late. When she heard that he'd been held up by the president, she would understand. Right? That was a totally good excuse for being late.

It was almost comical that he even cared what she thought. Wouldn't it have been fair to make her wait? Make her sweat it out? *She'd* been the one who cheated on *him*. The fact that it had happened more than two years ago and that he'd suggested they take some time off shouldn't have made any difference. Furthermore, she seemed to be more pissed at him than vice versa. Bedfellows made for strange politics.

He headed for the National Mall on foot. The former green space where protestors had once flourished was now home to dozens of restaurants and retail stores. Some Debbie Downers thought it was an eyesore, sneeringly calling the national park the "National Outlet Mall." Which was absurd, really: There wasn't an outlet store within a mile of the National Mall. It was strictly upscale chains. Trump's National Mall Glamorization Plan didn't allow discount retailers, dollar stores, or Macy's.

Jimmie glanced over his shoulder. For a second there, he thought he'd heard footsteps matching his. Was he being followed? He didn't recognize anyone or see anyone acting out of the ordinary.

The meeting with Trump on the Lincoln Bedroom deck had ratcheted his paranoia up a few notches. Hadn't the "leak" already been plugged? Lester Dorset was dead. Did Trump suspect Chris Christie was also an SJW sympathizer?

Cat would help him sort it all out. She could tell him if there was some sort of prior connection between Lester and the prime suspect for his murder, Corey Lewandowski. Right now, the only evidence tying the press secretary to Lester's death was circumstantial. Jimmie was putting together the puzzle, but there were still pieces missing.

He picked up his pace, weaving around the human tortoises jamming up the sidewalk. Tourists to the left of him, townies to the right. The restaurant was less than a mile away, but it would take him an hour if the sidewalks continued to be this clogged.

He spotted a pedicab parked on the edge of the National Mall. While people weren't stepping aside for Jimmie, they would have to if a pedicab was barreling their way.

A slim white guy was sitting on the pedicab's bicycle seat, checking his phone. He looked like Pee-wee Herman, if Pee-wee Herman was super into P90X. Jimmie could smell the pot from a mile away, but the kid's sculpted calves told him that he was all business.

Jimmie hopped into the back seat of the pedicab.

"Cracker Barrel," Jimmie said.

"Which one?" the kid said. "The restaurant on the National Mall, or the world's largest barrel of crackers?"

"The world's largest barrel of crackers is in Cedar Rapids."

"Yeah, it'd be quite a ride, I guess."

Jimmie tried not to roll his eyes. He clarified that, yes, he meant the restaurant and not a roadside attraction in the middle of the country.

The pedicab lurched forward. The kid rang the bell on his handlebars, and people began turning their heads and then stepping to the side. The pedicab started to gain momentum. If someone had been following Jimmie, they wouldn't be for much longer.

CHAPTER FORTY-THREE

★ ★ ★ ★

THE RITZ CRACKER BARREL

The pedicab driver may have been stoned out of his gourd, but he could peddle like a son of a bitch. The frightened pedestrians scattered when they saw him coming, much to Jimmie's delight.

"You go to school around here?" Jimmie shouted.

"Been out of school for a while," the kid said. "What do you do at the White House?"

Jimmie was confused at first, then realized he'd left his badge hanging around his neck. "Can't really say. Kind of top secret. Nothing exciting, though."

"Huh. I came pretty close to getting a job there, once."

"Internships can be competitive," Jimmie said, thinking back to the interviewing process for interns at the *Daily Blabber*. It had resembled Greek hazings more than proper job interviews. He'd never been involved in it, but he'd seen the photos of the interns in humiliating positions that were forwarded around the office. They'd made those photos of Iraqi prisoners look like child's play.

"Wasn't an internship I was competing for," the kid said, flying past a Ralph Lauren. "It was the vice presidency."

165

"The vice president of what?"

"Of the United States, man. Ended up as speaker of the—" They swung around a corner and nearly collided with a mother pushing a stroller. The pedicab went off the sidewalk and onto the grass. The kid's strong legs kept peddling, and they were back onto the sidewalk in no time.

The kid peddling had lost track of their conversation. Jimmie decided not to ask any more questions of him. He was so high, he thought he'd made a run for the White House! Jimmie had gotten stoned before, but never *that* stoned. Even a political newbie like Jimmie knew you had to be thirty-five to be president. He assumed the same rules applied to the vice presidency. There was no way this young buck was over twenty-five.

Instead of making small talk with the highest kite in the park, Jimmie ran over what he was going to say to Cat in his head: *I'm onto the story of the century. ALL the centuries. There's either a massive conspiracy against the president . . . or he's pulling the strings. You heard that right: There's a scandal going on at some of the highest levels of government . . . and I'm right in the middle of it. And I need your help.*

The kid rolled the pedicab to a stop in front of the Cracker Barrel just as the sun was setting. A row of empty, gold-plated rocking chairs on the porch rocked gently back and forth in the breeze. This was no ordinary Cracker Barrel—this was the fanciest one in the country. The Ritz Cracker Barrel.

"What do I owe you?" Jimmie asked.

"Don't worry about it," the kid said. "I do this for the exercise when Congress isn't in session. See you 'round, man."

Jimmie entered the restaurant and told the hostess he was meeting Cat. The woman ran down the list of tables. "She hasn't arrived yet, sir, but if you'll wait a moment, we'll have you seated."

Hasn't arrived yet? he thought. *That's strange . . .*

His phone buzzed in his pocket. Speak of the devil—Cat was calling him. He answered, "Just got here. Want me to order some biscuits for you?"

"That won't be necessary," a man on the other end of the line said. He had a slight twang to his voice that was difficult to place. "Skip the buttermilk biscuits . . . if you ever want to see your girlfriend alive again."

CHAPTER FORTY-FOUR

★ ★ ★ ★

A VERY PARTICULAR
SET OF SKILLS

"**S**he's not my girlfriend."

It was the wrong thing to say, but it was the first thing that came to Jimmie.

There was a pause at the other end of the line. For a second, he thought his phone had dropped the call. Then the mystery man spoke up: "This is Jimmie Bernwood, right? Do I have the correct number?"

"Yeah, it's me. I'm just saying, she's not my girlfriend."

"Cat Diaz," the man said. "You were meeting her at the Ritz Cracker Barrel."

"Right," Jimmie said. "I'm not disputing that. I'm just—"

"Your girlfriend, your date. Same thing."

"It wasn't a date," Jimmie said. "It's like a friends thing. No—more like a coworkers thing, I guess."

"You're taking her to the most romantic restaurant in the city on a Friday night, and you're telling me it wasn't supposed to be a date?"

"No! I mean, we never discussed it."

"Were you going to pay for her? If you were, that's a date. I can't believe she'd say yes to eating there if she didn't . . ."

Jimmie heard the man whisper to someone else in the room. "On a Friday night, right? Yeah, that's what I said." The voice got louder as the man spoke into the phone again. "Well, regardless of which one of you is in denial, we have her. And she's cute! Have you even asked if she likes you like that?"

The hostess had a couple of menus and was waiting on Jimmie. He held up a finger. Not that one. His index finger. "I need to take this," he whispered. "I'll be right back."

"Who are you talking to?" the man on the phone demanded.

Jimmie made his way through the other customers waiting in the foyer, the poor schmucks who didn't have reservations. Some of them could be waiting hours on standby, on the off-chance a table opened up. The Ritz Cracker Barrel filled up weeks in advance. There were some perks to orange-level security clearance.

"Sorry about that," he told the kidnapper. "So Cat is my ex. And I understand you have her?"

"Oh, that makes sense now. Yes, and if you don't give us what we want, you'll never see her again."

Somebody was taping this call right now: the White House, the NSA, Homeland Security. Somebody. The question, however, was whether or not anybody would listen to the recording in time for it to mean a damn thing to Cat. Even if they had a real-time eavesdropper from some shadowy government organization, the chances of them tracing it and sending the Navy SEALs to the kidnapper's door were miniscule. There was a good chance Jimmie was going to have to handle this situation himself.

"Are you still there, Mr. Bernwood?"

"I don't know who you are," he said. "I don't know what you want. If you're looking for ransom, I don't have a lot of money. What I do have, however, is a very particular set of skills . . . skills I have picked up over a very long career. Skills that can make me your worst nightmare. Let my daughter go now, and I won't come after you. But if you don't . . . I will find you. I will find you, and I will cause you pain. Unimaginable pain."

"Did you say she's your daughter? You're dating your daughter?"

"No, I didn't mean 'daughter.' I meant my date. No, wait, I didn't mean that either—"

"You think you're the first person I've tried to extract ransom from who's used that speech from *Taken*?" the man said. "I'm more than familiar with the skills you possess, Mr. Bernwood—meager as they are."

Jimmie sighed. "Tell me what you want. Get it over with."

"Don't get discouraged," the man said. His voice was flat. "We want the tapes."

"Like, sex tapes? I don't do that kind of journalism anymore."

"The Dorset tapes."

The only ones who knew about the tapes were Trump, Lester . . . and the Socialist Justice Warriors. The caller had just revealed his affiliation. Jimmie had snubbed the SJWs. Now they weren't asking him to help them—they were telling him he had to. Or else.

"We know you have them in your possession," the kidnapper continued.

"Let's say I did have these tapes. Is what's on them worth going to prison for? Because that's exactly what's going to happen to you once the Secret Service tracks you down. They're tracing this call right now."

The man laughed heartily.

"Is that funny to you?" Jimmie said.

"If you knew everything that we know, you'd be laughing too."

"What do you think is on these tapes?"

"Just bring them to us."

"Where are you?" Jimmie asked. "Clinton Plaza?"

"When you have the tapes in your possession, put a potted fern out on your patio at the Watergate. We will be in touch with further instructions. You have until midnight on Sunday."

"Can I have until midnight on Monday? It's a holiday weekend."

There was a pause on the other end of the line. It sounded like the man was whispering to someone in the background.

"Fine, Monday at midnight," the caller said. "Just put a fern out. Got that? A fern, Mr. Bernwood. And one last thing: Get the FBI or the CIA or even the FDA involved, and we kill your daughter."

"You mean my date."

"I thought it wasn't a date?"

"Okay, sure, maybe deep down I was hoping—"

The line went dead.

CHAPTER FORTY-FIVE

★ ★ ★ ★

TABLE FOR ONE

Jimmie reentered the restaurant. The hostess flashed a friendly smile. "Finished with your phone call, Mr. Bernwood?"

"I am," he said. "But I'll be dining alone tonight."

Although it seemed a tad insensitive to Cat to keep his reservation, Jimmie thought it would be what she wanted. Plus, the kidnappers had given him until Monday night to meet their demands. There was plenty of time to stuff his face with some old-fashioned southern-style cooking while he debated the most prudent course of action.

The smell of the made-from-scratch buttermilk biscuits had also been calling his name. He opened the menu. He had to focus. Review his options. Not the options on the menu—he already knew what he was going to order. But his options with regards to the kidnappers. He was out of his league, but that had never stopped him before.

The safest course of action was to cooperate with the kidnappers . . . for now. Getting the recorder out of the White House wasn't going to be easy, though. If it was, he'd have already done it. The Trump administration was so overrun with paranoia that they didn't let bags in or out of the building. No backpacks, no laptop cases, no purses, no briefcases. Not even fanny packs were allowed, which had to piss off Chef Fieri.

After he'd stuffed himself on his second order of complimentary buttermilk biscuits and was awaiting his third, the hostess arrived with another menu. "Your date is here, Mr. Bernwood," she said.

"That's . . . not possible," he stammered.

Emma Blythe stepped out from behind the hostess and took the seat across from Jimmie. She was wearing a tight, red cocktail dress that accentuated her curves. She looked like she'd just stepped out of a noir novel and into his life.

"Hello, darling," Emma said. "I hope you've saved room for dessert."

CHAPTER FORTY-FIX

★ ★ ★ ★

THE SEVENTH-LEADING CAUSE OF DEATH IN THE US

Emma took one sip of the iced tea she'd ordered and made a horrible retching sound. "Dear God, that's awful. I always forget you Americans put sugar in your tea."

"Don't look at me—I'm from the Midwest," Jimmie said. "Sweet tea is a southern thing."

"Is diabetes also a southern thing?"

"One would assume so, what with obesity rates being so high in southern states." Jimmie picked up his phone and Googled *states with highest rates of diabetes*. "Damn, would you look at that. Says here that nine of the top ten states with the highest rates of type 2 diabetes *are* in the—"

Emma snatched the phone out of his hand and dropped it into the last of his bowl of creamy tomato soup. He'd dunked enough phones underwater over the years to know that it wasn't worth diving in after. It also wasn't the first time he'd had his phone taken away by a woman at dinner.

"I would have put it away, had you asked," he said.

174

"I could care less about your lack of table etiquette. I had to make sure the NSA wasn't listening to every word of our conversation."

"They might be interested in the seventh-leading cause of death in this country," Jimmie said. "You never know."

"While public health statistics are endlessly fascinating to someone, somewhere, that's not what I came to talk to you about. You're going to tell me what sort of mess you've gotten yourself into." She paused. "A word of warning, however: Leave anything out, and I'll know you're lying. You'll be arrested for attempted espionage."

"How will you know if I leave anything out, though?"

"Maybe I will. Maybe I won't. Are you willing to risk it?"

He leaned across the table. "A woman's life is at stake here."

"Millions of lives are at stake here," Emma shot back. "*Billions* of lives, possibly. We're talking about the office of the president of the United States of America. Do you not understand that? This is far bigger than one person's life. No matter how much you want to shag her."

Jimmie saw that his tie had taken a dip in his soup, and he wiped it on the tablecloth. "It's such bullshit for you to bring that up. Why couldn't I just care about another human being for altruistic reasons?"

"It would certainly be a first," she said. "I'm surprised you even know what the word 'altruism' means."

"I'm full of surprises," he said, even though she was seeing right through him at practically every turn.

Their waiter brought their entrées out and went to pick up the empty bowl in front of Jimmie. Or nearly empty, except for the dead phone coated in tomato soup.

"Sir . . . there's a phone in your soup," the waiter said. "Would you like me to fish it out?"

"It's not mine," Jimmie said coolly.

"I am so sorry. Let me apologize on behalf of the Ritz Cracker Barrel."

Jimmie stared him in the eyes. "Take it off my bill, or I'm going to Yelp."

The waiter hurried off. Emma stared at Jimmie as if he'd just shit on the rug.

"What?"

"You're quite something," she said.

"Quite charming?"

"Quite *something*," she repeated.

While Jimmie picked over his chicken-fried chicken, he told Emma everything. To get information, you had to give up information. He wasn't sure why he trusted her, but he did. It might have also had something to do with the fact that Jimmie was strangely deferential to women in positions of authority over him. It was a weakness. But he would be strong. Even though he'd been daydreaming about making love to Emma on the beanbag chair Biden had left behind in the VP's West Wing office, he would be strong. He wasn't about to get into another mess like he'd gotten into with Cat.

The fact that Emma had arrived just twenty minutes after the kidnappers had hung up on him had to mean someone had alerted her to the call—the NSA or Homeland Security. She'd been watching him closely.

Jimmie didn't think she'd come here to put the screws on him, though. It wasn't like she was going to just pull out a gun and murder him right there in the middle of the Ritz Cracker Barrel. Though that would have been a pretty baller move.

"So that's where we're at," Jimmie said after finishing his tale. "I've turned over all the cards I have. Now it's your turn."

"Is that how you think this works?" Emma said. "Tell me something, James: Were you planning to leak all this to Cat Diaz? Is that why you were meeting her tonight?"

"I signed a nondisclosure."

"That you planned to break for the right price."

"Are you going to fire me?"

Emma sipped her sweet tea. Slowly. Deliberately.

"No," she said.

"No?"

"I'm going to help you get your girlfriend back. In exchange, you are going to drop this amateur little 'investigation' of yours. If the press secretary did throw Lester off the roof, it wouldn't make a bit of difference. You'd still have to pin it on him. Surveillance tapes from that far back have already been wiped. All you've got is a hunch."

"Sometimes, that's all you need."

"Sometimes," Emma said. "But not this time. Remember that Lewandowski manhandled that reporter on the campaign trail *on video* and walked away without any charges."

"There's a corpse buried somewhere on the White House grounds, and you're telling me to forget about it?"

"That's exactly what I'm telling you."

Jimmie sighed. It was an overly dramatic, sort of bitchy sigh. Totally warranted, however. She was asking him to *give up on a story?* Once he got his claws into something, it was difficult for him to let go. He was like a tick, digging in for the long haul while he drew blood. Could he let go . . . for Cat's sake? He'd have to think about that.

Jimmie said, "So you, what, trace the call and have Trump send in the Navy SEALs to rescue her? How does this work?"

"The president would never authorize the use of the military to rescue a kidnapped reporter, and you know it," Emma said. "Even against the SJWs. And it wouldn't make a bit of difference to appeal to President Trump's romantic side. He'd just tell you to get another girlfriend—one who doesn't go around getting herself kidnapped. Officially, the US government won't be intervening. We don't negotiate with terrorists. Unofficially . . . I would like to see this situation resolved as quickly as possible. There's been enough bloodshed at the White House in recent weeks, wouldn't you agree?"

Jimmie nodded but didn't say anything. He had a mouthful of fried apples.

"Just because the US government isn't going to do a bloody thing about your friend doesn't mean you're out of luck," Emma said. "They're not the only government in the world, you know."

"The Russians," he said.

"The Brits," she said.

"But we're on the verge of war with the UK. Why would they lift a finger?"

"Because I'm not just the apprentice," Emma said. "I'm with MI6—the Secret Intelligence Service."

CHAPTER FORTY-SEVEN

★ ★ ★ ★

NINETY PERCENT OF THE TIME

So Trump had been right about there being a leak in the White House after all. He probably had never imagined how high ranking the leak was, however. The apprentice was as close to the Oval Office as you could get—both figuratively and literally. And Trump never would know, because Jimmie wasn't anybody's informant. Not even the president's.

He had to tip his cap to the United Kingdom. The British intelligence community must have predicted Trump's rise to power and placed an operative close to him in the eventuality he ascended to the US presidency.

The British had always been much smarter than the United States. Part of that was the accent, of course. Part of it, however, was that they'd just been playing this game much longer than their American counterparts had. They literally had hundreds of years more institutional knowledge baked into their psyche than the relatively young upstarts on this side of the Atlantic did. Funny, then, that they'd already dropped two wars to the United States, but hey—any given Sunday.

"Call in your British SEALs or whatever," Jimmie said begrudgingly, tossing his napkin on the table. "Forget the story—we need to save her. I'm ready when you are."

"Hold on," Emma said. "We don't have 'British SEALs.' MI6's elite special-ops force is the Royal OTTERs. Unfortunately, they're all busy preparing to guard the home front in case this war between our countries actually breaks out. Our best option here is to cooperate with the kidnappers."

A waiter arrived with a fresh glass of sweet tea for Emma. Despite her avowed distaste for the beverage, she was now on her fourth refill.

When the waiter was gone, Jimmie said, "You trust these Socialist Justice Warriors?"

"Real-life kidnappers aren't like the ones in Hollywood movies. If they say they're going to trade you for someone, they're probably going to keep their word—as long as you follow through with your end of the bargain. Ninety percent of the time, nobody gets hurt. Except for maybe a cut-off finger or toe, which they mail to you to show you they're serious. In this case, there's not enough time for them to mail you any appendages. Even if they overnighted her ring finger, say, there's no guarantee you'd get it. Holiday weekends cause massive postal delays."

Ninety percent of the time, nobody gets hurt. What about the other ten percent?

He said, "I'm surprised you want to hand the recorder over."

"I've worked with Trump long enough to know he doesn't say anything in private that he wouldn't say in public," she said. "You were right: Lester Dorset was a bloody fool."

"Finally, somebody agrees with me."

"You're also a bloody fool, but for different reasons," Emma said.

Was she teasing him? He'd have time to tease her back later.

"You're sure I need to drop this whole Lester story, though?" he asked.

"If there really was a story here capable of bringing the administration to its knees, I would have exposed it long ago," Emma said. "I'm doing everything I can to keep Trump in check and avoid this idiotic 'three-peat' he keeps going on about. You've been to the Security Council meetings. If it was up to Trump and the rest of those wankers, the UK would be a pile of rubble right now. I might just be the only person standing in his way. If you try to pin the murder on Lewandowski, and he doesn't confess, who do you think people are going to point fingers at next? The Brit in the White House."

"I guess you're right," Jimmie said.

"Are you pouting?"

"No," he lied. "So we need to figure out how to get the recorder out of the White House, then."

"You'd never get it past security on your own," she said. "With my help, however, it will be a breeze. Only a handful of people in the administration can walk in and out of the building without being frisked . . . including the apprentice."

Jimmie shoveled another biscuit into his mouth, even though he'd felt full fifteen minutes ago. He was simply stress-eating at this point. Jimmie could see his story about Lester's body—and whatever scandal was beneath it—blowing Emma's cover in some way. She was just trying to throw water on the flames. From Jimmie's perspective, though, the fire was out of control.

Emma said, "I'll pick up the tab, and we can head back to the White House. Where's the recorder?"

"A safe place. I might need your help getting to it, though."

"You have the same clearance level as the president, remember?"

He nodded. "But there are some places that might raise some eyebrows, were I to walk in without an appointment. Especially after business hours on a Friday night."

"I seriously doubt that."

"So I can just walk into the Lincoln Bedroom, you're saying?"

She frowned. "That . . . might be a problem."

"I know that the president and first lady were taking off for Florida tonight—"

"I watched the helicopter take off for the airport. Still, it would be suspicious for you to just go creeping around in the family quarters while they're away."

"Have you ever thought about all the presidents who've had sex in that bedroom?"

"It's the guest bedroom," she said.

"So?"

Emma continued, "We'll have to come up with a good reason for you to . . . for you to . . ."

Emma winced and grabbed her stomach. It looked like she had felt a sharp pain, as if she'd just been kicked in the gut by an invisible foot. She hadn't touched her food, though—must have been too much sweet tea. Caffeine could irritate an ulcer something wicked.

Emma started rocking back and forth in her chair while staring blankly into the distance. This was no ulcer.

Jimmie looked around for a waiter—she needed medical attention.

Emma thrust a hand out to steady herself, grabbing a bunch of tablecloth. She clutched it tight just as she tipped backward, taking her chair and the tablecloth to the ground. Their plates and silverware crashed to the floor.

Her glass, however, was still standing.

While time had seemed to slow down, it now sped back up. Jimmie shot out of his chair and knelt beside her. She wasn't trembling anymore.

In fact, she wasn't even breathing anymore.

Either she'd just died of sudden-onset type 2 diabetes from her sweet tea . . . or she'd been poisoned.

CHAPTER FORTY-EIGHT

★ ★ ★ ★

STORMING THE CASTLE

The White House guard patted Jimmie down and waved him through. "You forgot your phone in your office?" the guard said. "Jesus, I'd leave my dick somewhere 'fore I left my phone."

Jimmie snorted. He hadn't needed a cover story about returning to the White House to pick up his phone, but he couldn't very well tell the truth: that he was here for a heist.

After Emma Blythe had croaked on the floor of the Ritz Cracker Barrel, he'd backed up slowly from her lifeless body—first in horror and then in panic mode. Whoever had poisoned her drink could have been coming for him next.

Commotion spread fast across the celebrity-packed restaurant. While Dr. Oz shrieked in panic from under a table, George Clooney leapt forward to administer CPR to Emma's lifeless body. But there was no bringing her back. Not even George Clooney could breathe life back into the former Miss Universe.

So Jimmie had backed off, slowly at first. Onlookers were more concerned with taking selfies with Clooney and the unconscious woman than with watching the man she'd been dining with. When he'd backed up all the way to the edge of the dining area, he'd spun around and bolted out the door.

The crowds on the sidewalk had thinned considerably. He ran until he was out of breath, and then he jogged. It wasn't until the White House was in view that he realized he'd dined and dashed. It was a miracle he hadn't been shot and killed by a good hillbilly Samaritan, like so many others who had tried the same stunt at Cracker Barrels across the country.

Jimmie held his badge up to the door inside the Reagan Library. The lock clicked open. His clearance level hadn't been restricted . . . yet. It occurred to him that this could be the last time he ever set foot inside the White House. He couldn't hide the fact that he'd been at dinner with a British spy. Clooney wouldn't testify against him, but somebody at the Ritz Cracker Barrel would. If he wasn't just buried in the backyard with Lester by the time of his trial.

The one good thing about Emma biting it, he supposed, was that he was no longer beholden to squash the story about Lester's death. There was that shadowy figure on the GIF, which cast major doubt on Trump's version of events. Cat, with her intimate knowledge of Lester, would provide the missing pieces to the puzzle. She was a great editor—she'd always seen the holes in his stories that he was too close to see. All he had to do was trade the worthless recorder to the SJWs for her.

Jimmie took the subbasement's service elevator to the second floor. While it didn't go all the way to the third floor, the elevator at least got him into the family quarters as stealthily as possible.

He stepped off the elevator and into a long service corridor. It appeared to run adjacent to the length of the State Dining Room. He passed a white sign reading REMEMBER: COOK MEAT BEFORE SERVING!!! taped to the wall next to a stack of boxes labeled TACO BOWLS. He spotted a tray of silver-ware and paused to pocket a serrated knife. It might come in handy if the Lincoln Bedroom was locked.

Or if you run into trouble, he thought darkly.

He entered the dining room. In the center of the tables were cornucopias, packed with what looked to be every product made by Little Debbie. He poked his head into the hallway outside. To his left were the Green, Red, and Blue Rooms—or, since Trump had ordered them redecorated, the 10K, 14K, and 24K Rooms. To his right were the stairs that led up to the presidential bedrooms on the renovated third floor. The only problem was the Secret Service flunky standing guard. The hairless one.

Jimmie closed the door. He hadn't been expecting the Secret Service up here, since the president was halfway to Mar-a-Lago by now. Even in the prez's absence, though, they probably still had to guard the living quarters. Wouldn't want any wayward busboys sneaking off with a pair of presidential boxers. Talk about illegal briefs.

Jimmie searched the room for something to distract the Secret Service agent. The agents were generally unflappable, but Jimmie had one thing going for him: It was almost nine o'clock. That meant it was nearing the end of the agent's shift. He had to be mentally clocked out already. How to distract him, how to distract—

Jimmie snatched a handful of cut flowers from a vase on the nearest table. He could . . . offer them to the Secret Service agent? Ridiculous. The man out there was a legit trained killer. He might just take a shot at Jimmie for the hell of it, should he come at him with flowers like some peace-loving hippie.

Jimmie hoisted the ceramic vase. It was heavy enough to knock the agent out, if he ran at him fast enough and clocked him across the side of the skull. While Jimmie wasn't the quickest cat around, he had the element of surprise on his side.

Unfortunately, he'd also end up serving time for assaulting a federal agent if he was caught. And he would be caught, whenever the next agent showed up for their shift. He set the vase down on the table. The table . . .

No, not the table. The table*cloth.*

They think the family quarters are haunted.

Jimmie used the knife to cut two eyeholes in it. He threw the white cloth over his head. It draped down, covering his body. He looked at his reflection in the metallic vase.

He looked exactly like a person wearing an ill-fitting sheet. In the hallway, to a pair of tired eyes filtered through sunglasses, he might look more like a ghost.

Or a member of the KKK, you nitwit.

He didn't have much choice. He just hoped the agent wouldn't try to shoot him, because that would suck. He didn't want to get shot—not tonight. Not ever, but definitely not tonight. He had to get his girl back (not that she was his girl again, not yet) and possibly pull the sheets off the largest scandal Washington had ever seen.

CHAPTER FORTY-NINE

★ ★ ★

SOMETHING STRANGE
IN THE NEIGHBORHOOD

Jimmie stepped into the hallway. He could just make out the Secret Service agent through the eyeholes. Jimmie slouched down and raised his arms inside the sheet. The agent, standing guard some twenty yards away, took no notice.

"OooOooOooOooooOOoOOOO," Jimmie moaned.

Grow Some Fucking Eyebrows swung his head in Jimmie's direction. There was a deeply unamused expression on his face.

Jimmie froze. He'd suddenly lost his bravado. This was, undoubtedly, the height of his stupidity. He'd done some dumb things before, but this one took the Little Debbie snack cake.

The agent lowered his sunglasses to get a better look at the phantasm.

Jimmie waved his outstretched hands from side to side, swaying in the hallway as if he were at a USA Freedom Girls for America concert.

The agent stared at him. Either the man was frightened to his very core, or he was in such a state of disbelief that he couldn't move a muscle.

"OooOoOOOOooOOO," Jimmie said, getting his nerve back. "OoooOoOoOOOooooOOo."

The agent finally pushed his sunglasses back into place. "Very funny, Junior," he said. "Now get to bed. Your dad wouldn't be very happy to hear you were up this late."

Jimmie dropped his arms. *Junior?* Of course. The agent thought he was Donald Trump Jr. up past his bedtime. This was the first that Jimmie had heard about the forty-year-old still living at home, but why not? If Jimmie's parents lived in the White House, he'd do the same.

He walked past the agent and hiked up the tablecloth so that he didn't trip while walking up the steps. The agent grabbed him by the arm and spun him around.

This ghost just got busted.

Jimmie tried to inhale deeply to steady himself, but all he could take were quick and shallow breaths. His heart was pounding now like a hotel bed against a wall. The agent had a hold on him and was staring through his eyeholes, just inches away.

"No Xbox, you hear me?" the agent said. "You need your sleep. Big day tomorrow."

If Jimmie didn't respond, he'd be unmasked for sure; if he said something, even a word, the agent would discover his ruse.

He looked the agent in the eyes . . . and stomped his Oxfords in protest.

"I don't make the rules, kiddo," the agent said, letting him go.

Jimmie stomped his way up the stairs, playing the part of the petulant Trump child to a T. When he reached the third floor, he turned down the hall and ditched the tablecloth behind a potted plant.

From the closed door nearest him, he heard a full artillery at work: machine-gun fire, grenades. *Human Hiroshima 3: Soldier of Misfortune*, if he wasn't mistaken. Somebody was disobeying daddy. If he was anything like the gamers Jimmie had known in college, Junior wouldn't be getting up for a good long while—not even to use the restroom. Jimmie was thankful he'd only ever been a casual gamer. He could stop any time he wanted—and he had stopped, when he'd pawned his PlayStation to pay off his parking tickets. And then pawned his Xbox after his car got towed when he double-parked outside the ticket-payment office.

Jimmie straightened his tie and ran a hand through his short-cropped hair. He strutted down the hall. So this is what James Bond felt like. A little tipsier, probably, but there's a swagger that begins to course through your veins when you're firing on all cylinders. James Bond . . . Jimmie Bernwood. They even shared the same initials. They also shared them with Justin Bieber, but Jimmie wasn't quite ready to proclaim himself the next Biebs.

He paused at the doorway to the Lincoln Bedroom. The door was cracked an inch. He looked to his left and to his right down the hallway to confirm he was still alone and then slipped inside the Lincoln Bedroom.

Moonlight filtered in through the spacious glass doors that opened onto the veranda. The sliver of light shone directly onto the desk, where a handwritten copy of the Trump Address was laid out on permanent display. Next to it sat the recorder.

He felt his way along the wall toward the desk. If he'd planned this out, he would have brought a flashlight with him.

If he'd had his phone, he could have used a flashlight app, even. But he didn't have time to plan. He didn't even have time to use the restroom (which he badly needed to do).

Jimmie picked up the recorder. He could barely believe it was real, but it was. A sense of relief rushed through him. He still had to figure out a way to get the damned recorder *out* of the White House, but the first part of his mission was complete. Mission impossible? As W would say, "Mission accomplished"!

But just like George W. Bush had learned, you should never celebrate before the end of a mission, even if the end is within sight. Before he could even turn around for the door, a woman's voice rang out from the darkness:

"Took you long enough, Mr. Jimmie."

CHAPTER FIFTY

★ ★ ★

VICTORIA'S SECRET

Jimmie Bernwood recognized the woman's husky voice. Her Eastern European accent was unmistakable.

"Mrs. Trump," he said, slipping the recorder into his pants pocket. He turned around. With a fuller moon, he might have been able to see her more clearly on the bed. As it was, he only saw her outline. And what a fine outline it was.

"Call me Victoria," she said, pronouncing it *Veek-toria*.

"I didn't know you were here," Jimmie said. "I thought you'd gone to Florida."

"Mar-a-Lago?" she said. "Donny took Mr. Christie. They're going to golf all weekend. And who knows what else."

Jimmie eyed the door. His first instinct was to bolt for it. Get the hell out of here. Unfortunately, he couldn't just run out of the White House. His aching ribs couldn't take another beating.

"I was in here talking to your husband earlier and left something behind," he said. "Sorry to disturb you."

"The little tape machine."

He swallowed hard. "The recorder. Yes."

"I assume you have found it," she said, "or else you are very happy to see me."

Jimmie glanced down at his pants. The recorder bulged unseemly in his pocket.

She asked, "Are you happy to see me, Mr. Jimmie? I have been thinking about your big hands ever since our little flirtation earlier this week."

Victoria flipped on the bedside lamp. Jimmie felt his breath hitch as he got a good look at the first lady, who was sitting upright against the headboard. The bedsheet and comforter had been tossed aside, giving him a full view of the toned and tanned body that had graced so many magazine covers over the years. Her lacy, black bra-and-panties set left little up to the imagination. Jimmie had spent enough time with her racy *National Review* spread to fill in the missing pieces.

Still, he had to control himself. The first lady was toying with him like a cat with a mouse. If he wasn't careful, he'd end up decapitated on the porch by morning.

He cleared his throat. "Are you trying to seduce me?"

She slowly traced her full, luscious lips with her tongue. "I'm not trying to seduce you—I *am* seducing you."

"Your husband—"

"Isn't here."

"He's the president. If he found out I was even in his wife's bedroom . . ."

"Why do you think I'm sleeping in the guest bedroom?"

"Do you always sleep wearing lingerie? I would imagine the underwire isn't very comfortable."

She giggled. "I usually sleep naked. *Very* naked."

Jimmie had no idea how one could be "very naked" as opposed to simply "naked," but he was sufficiently intrigued. Now there were two bulges in his pants.

What the hell are you doing? his rational side chimed in. *Sure, you're "intrigued" by the prospect of seeing this gorgeous woman in the nude. But what woman* aren't *you "intrigued" by? Remember that you're doing this to save Cat from the kidnappers. You're risking your livelihood—right here, right now—for the woman you used to love. And also the woman you need to help you complete the puzzle of Lester's death.*

Jimmie said, "Listen, I know it can't be easy, being married to the president of the United States—hell, it can't be easy being married at all. I've never walked the aisle myself. I thought I'd found the right girl once, but then things fell apart. I might have found her again—but it all depends on me getting this recorder to the bad guys who've kidnapped her."

"What a shame," she said. Victoria's fingers went to the front of her push-up bra. She unhooked its clasp. The bra split in two, releasing her breasts from their captivity. The bra hadn't been a push-up bra after all: Her breasts seemed to float before her in defiance of gravitational laws. The natural order of things might have been put temporarily on hold, actually, as Jimmie had sucked all the air out of the room.

Y'know, he thought, *I'm not* actually *dating Cat right now.*

Yes, he was going to rescue her from the bad guys, and blah, blah, blah. But until they actually started seeing each other again, it meant they were free to see other people. Right? When else was he going to get the chance to hop into bed with a supermodel of indeterminate age in the Lincoln Bedroom? He could practically sense Lincoln's ghost in the room, telling him to hit that shit.

He dropped his voice to a whisper: "Aren't there, like, video cameras all over the place?"

"Is that what my husband told you? Ha! There are no cameras in the bedrooms."

"What about the restrooms?"

"You want to do it in the restroom? I knew you were a little pervert when I saw you watching me, Mr. Jimmie."

"The bed is fine," he said, loosening his tie.

CHAPTER FIFTY-ONE

⭐ ⭐ ⭐ ⭐

IT HAPPENS TO PLENTY OF GUYS

As Victoria unbuttoned Jimmie's pants, another wave of hesitation hit him. It had nothing to do with Cat or with the fact that Victoria Trump was married to the president. He knew that she was just using him to get back at her husband. She'd praised Jimmie's "big hands," but they both knew they were just average. To someone who's starving, though, a crumb looks like a meal.

What was causing him to have second thoughts was the fact that *a White House sex scandal was unfolding before his very eyes . . . and he didn't care.* This despite a story here just as salacious as anything he'd reported at the *Daily Blabber.* Although he'd never cared for politics, Donald J. Trump and the first lady were undoubtedly celebrities: Trump's marital troubles with past wives had driven dirt sheet sales in the eighties and nineties. Who could forget his first wife confronting his mistress on the slopes in Colorado? The lengthy prenup battle with Marla Maples? Or the blink-and-you've-missed-it marriage to Megyn Kelly?

The story unzipping below Jimmie's belt was *bigger* than all that. Even if he hadn't been personally involved, the first couple were clearly having some sort of marital difficulties. Who knew how long Victoria and her husband been sleeping in separate bedrooms? Jimmie should have felt something. Anything. Well, anything besides the hand massaging him, which he *definitely* felt.

But no. A Trump sex scandal was small boobies compared to the rising body count at the White House. As much as it pained Jimmie to admit, whatever conspiracy was unfolding around him outside of the Lincoln Bedroom ran far deeper than what was happening inside the Lincoln Bedroom.

He never thought he'd think that there could be anything bigger than a sex scandal. But he'd found one—one that excited his journalistic instincts. One that got his blood boiling. Lester Dorset . . . the dead SJW . . . Emma Blythe being poisoned . . . the threat of war with America's closest ally . . . and the most powerful men and women in the world. Something big was brewing, something that dwarfed a little extramarital swapping of bodily fluids.

"I can't do this," Jimmie said, pulling away from Victoria. "I'm sorry."

She frowned at him. "Is it your kidnapped girlfriend?"

He nodded solemnly. It was only partially about Cat—and she wasn't his girlfriend—but, yeah. No reason to get Victoria involved in whatever nasty business was happening at the White House.

"I can help you," she said. "I want to help you."

He tucked his shirt in and buttoned his pants. "I can't get out of here with the recorder. But you can probably just walk out with it."

"If I leave, it will be suspicious. Donny doesn't like it when I leave."

A woman like Victoria didn't deserve to be locked up on the third floor of the White House like some crazy aunt who'd lost her mind. No woman deserved that. Not even crazy aunts.

Victoria needed someone who cared about her . . . somebody who wouldn't leave town to play golf all weekend while his wife and her amazing rack were stuck at home.

Jimmie gazed into her eyes and communicated all this with a single glance. She gazed back at him, letting him know she picked up what he was putting down.

He shot a glance at the window. The Rose Garden was directly below. If he exited the building through the rear employee entrance, he'd walk right past the flower garden on his way out. He'd be beyond the most invasive level of White House security at that point. All Victoria would have to do is toss the recorder out the window, and he'd catch it.

He glanced back at Victoria, who nodded. She understood his plan.

If things don't work out with my girl, I'll be back for you, Jimmie told Victoria with a wiggle of his eyebrows.

You promise? she asked with a narrowing of her eyes.

I promise, he said with a flare of his nostrils.

He bent down and kissed her on the forehead. They both knew he was lying, but they kept playing the parts. Jimmie knew that not only was it what James Bond would do . . . it was also, he realized with some horror, what Trump would do.

After his plan went off without a hitch, Jimmie Bernwood set the potted plant out on his deck at the Watergate. It had been a long day, but it was going to be an even longer weekend. He finally dozed off around one in the morning. He slept well and dreamt of large-breasted women.

Excerpt From the Trump/Dorset Sessions

July 1, 2018, 7:56 PM

DORSET: You believe in God.

TRUMP: Doesn't everybody?

DORSET: Atheists don't. Agnostics don't know.

TRUMP: They should. They really, really should. The Bible is one of the two greatest books ever written. Right up there with *The Art of the Deal*. I would say that Jesus is my favorite author, besides myself.

DORSET: Jesus didn't write the Bible.

TRUMP: Then He had a helluva ghostwriter. Shows you what a great manager He was.

DORSET: Manager?

TRUMP: He started his church with just twelve guys. Twelve! And look how many employees He has now. I have tremendous respect for the guy. He really knew how to work a room.

DORSET: Speaking of working rooms, you've come under fire repeatedly for working them into frenzies.

At one of your campaign stops, you pointed to the press corps and called them "scum." Journalists covering your campaign reported being pelted with batteries and ice cubes, among other objects.

TRUMP: That's not true.

DORSET: No? There's video of it . . .

TRUMP: It wasn't just one stop. It was multiple stops. It was a part of my routine for a while. The line about "scum" always got big laughs. Brought the house down. People loved the interactive part, with the batteries and whatnot.

DORSET: Since, by your own admission, the media actually helped you out, shouldn't you at least show them a little more respect now?

TRUMP: What do you want me to do, send Fox News a thank-you card? I'll send them a fuck-you card, because fuck you, Roger Ailes. Do they make fuck-you cards?

DORSET: I've never checked.

TRUMP: Someone could make an easy million selling fuck-you cards. They wouldn't even have to sell them on the street, because I'd buy every damn one. I'd have a long list of recipients, believe me. Longer than my Christmas card list, that's for sure. Who's in charge of making national holidays? Is that me?

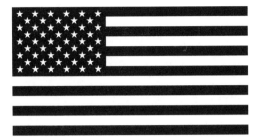

Saturday, September 1, 2018

CHAPTER FIFTY-TWO

★ ★ ★ ★

STUPID IS AS STUPID DOES

Jimmie Bernwood rose just after ten the next morning. He used the toilet and stretched his arms. He'd been up late at the White House, so he didn't get his regular ten hours of sleep. Any other Saturday, he might have lounged around in bed until noon. Unfortunately, he had too much to do this weekend to prepare for the swap.

He'd decided that he would make a copy of the recordings. Not because of their content, but because he might need them down the line as evidence. He also needed to buy a gun. With Trump's Affordable Arms Act, that would be relatively simple.

Jimmie toweled off his hands and—

He paused to stare in the mirror. There, on his forehead in black magic marker, was a message written across two lines: NOON. INT'L SPY MUSEUM. And running down the side of his cheek, as if someone had run out of space: OR SHE DIES.

Noon?! He couldn't believe what an idiot he'd been. Why had he set the plant out last night and not waited a day or two? What a stupid mistake.

He spun the dial on the safe.

The recorder was inside, untouched.

Curious that the SJWs sneaked into his hotel room to deliver a message but hadn't tried to force him into giving up the recorder. Why hadn't they tortured him? Maybe they weren't as villainous as they seemed . . . or maybe they just assumed Jimmie wouldn't have been so stupid as to bring his bargaining chip with him back to the hotel.

Well, guess what, bad guys? he thought. *I* am *that stupid.*

If they wanted to overestimate him, let them.

He glanced again at the clock. He had only a little over an hour and a half now to get to the International Spy Museum, which was at least a forty-minute bus ride away. No time to make a copy of the recordings. No time to pick up a gun for protection. He was heading into this thing with just his wits.

From past experience, those weren't going to be enough.

He flipped on the television as he got dressed. Emma Blythe's death should have been the lead story on CNN. Instead, the news network was running a story on gluten-free hip-hop. Nothing on Fox News, MSNBC, or the half a dozen other twenty-four-hour news channels either.

Someone was keeping her death quiet.

They couldn't do it forever, of course—this wasn't another Lester Dorset situation. Come Tuesday morning, the White House staff would be abuzz if she weren't in her office by nine. Was her killer also doing the cover-up? Or did somebody within the White House or the US intelligence community know she was a spy and thus was keeping a lid on her assassination until the full depth of her espionage was known?

On his way out to catch the bus, he passed the stack of Trump books he'd amassed. Hadn't had time to color them all just yet—maybe he never would, if he was gunned down today in the mean streets of the nation's capital. The book on top caught his eye, however: *Trump: The Art of the Deal: The Expanded Coloring Edition.*

Maybe Jimmie didn't have to go into his negotiation with the kidnappers unarmed after all.

CHAPTER FIFTY-THREE

★ ★ ★ ★

DRAWING CHICKENS

The International Spy Museum was located ten blocks east of the White House. Jimmie had read about the museum in a guide to area attractions. The private museum supposedly featured "the largest collection of international espionage artifacts ever placed on public display." The museum's board of directors included past members of the CIA, FBI, NSA, and even the KGB. In a city that supposedly had ten thousand spies, there were bound to be a few hanging out at the Spy Museum just shooting the shit. *This* was the place the kidnappers wanted to meet?

It seemed that Jimmie wasn't the only one who'd overestimated the opposition's intelligence. *It's your funeral, tough guys*, he thought as he paid the twenty-five bucks for entry.

The girl at the counter with the nose stud and pageboy haircut handed him his ticket. "Made it just in time," she said. "Nobody's going to die."

His heart stopped. "Excuse me?"

"The reminder on your face," she said. "Noon? You've got twelve minutes."

Of course. In his rush to get out the door, he'd forgotten to scrub the message from his face. The girl had read the backward message. Probably one of the skills you learned on the first day at a place like this.

"Is there a restroom I can use to wash it off?" Jimmie asked. "My roommate's always drawing shit on my face."

"Might be time for a new roommate."

"At least it wasn't a huge cock this time," he said, a little louder than he probably should have, what with all the children around. Because it was a Saturday, the families were out in full force. A father in the next line shot him a look of disapproval, which was absolutely warranted.

"My roommate, uh, is always drawing chickens," Jimmie explained, loudly and to nobody in particular. "Cocks, as everybody is well aware, are male chickens. That's what I'm talking about—not cocks as in male genitals—"

"Please stop talking," the girl behind the ticket counter said.

Jimmie headed down the hall. He'd nearly made a scene back there—not good, if he was trying to keep a low profile. The last thing he wanted to do was get tossed out of the museum and risk making the kidnappers think he'd bailed on them. Then what would happen to Cat?

After he washed the marker off, he realized he still had a few minutes to kill before noon. Plenty of time to do his morning business, which he'd skipped to get here on time.

All three stalls were open. Every time he encountered a choice of stalls at a public restroom, he had to do some quick mental gymnastics to determine which had the least germs. He wasn't phobic about germs or anything, but he wasn't a fool. It was automatically assumed that, in Western countries, most people would go for the stall farthest to the left. Stall #1. So he should pick stall #2 or #3. Except most people *knew* that most people would pick stall #1, so they would also go for the second or third stall . . . meaning that stall #1 would actually be the cleanest of the three. However, most people would run through the same calculation in their minds, leading them to choose stall #1 over the others because of its presumed cleanliness . . . meaning that, in the end, stall #1 would get the most traffic and have the most germs.

Jimmie chose the second stall as he always ended up doing. The third stall had never been in play, because everybody knew that the farthest stall to the right was the one where people went when they needed the most privacy—to shoot up drugs or drop a bomb.

He plopped himself down on the seat and opened the museum brochure he'd picked up at the gate. Somebody sat down in the stall to his right. Jimmie could see the man's white penny loafers under the divider. The man coughed. This confirmed Jimmie's impression that stall #1 was nothing but a germ farm.

He returned his attention to the brochure. According to the map, there were three floors at the museum. The permanent exhibits included "School for Spies" and "The Secret History of History" and apparently included interactive elements such as adopting your own spy name. Neat. There were a couple of different special exhibits going on right now, too, including one he wouldn't have minded checking out on the Bond girls. But one temporary exhibit in particular grabbed his eye: "Ten Years of *Taken*."

So that was why the kidnappers had chosen this as a meeting place. They wanted to mock his false bravado. They were in for a little surprise, though. He'd spent the bus ride over here boning up on his Trump negotiation tactics. He was ready for war.

CHAPTER FIFTY-FOUR

★ ★ ★ ★

STOOL FOR SPIES

Somebody opened the door to the third stall and sat down. Jimmie could see a pair of women's shoes underneath the stall divider. Nothing unusual about that—to each their own. This wasn't North Carolina.

What *did* strike him as unusual, however, was that the person to his left didn't drop their pants after sitting down on the toilet. Shooting up? Maybe. Stall three, man. What the hell.

Jimmie quickly finished his business. As he was zipping up, he heard the warbling of a sparrow. No, not a sparrow—a house finch. It was the same chirping call he'd heard in Clinton Plaza just before Connor approached him.

Either there were birds on the loose in the museum's restroom, or the Socialist Justice Warriors had found him. Apparently the drop zone was going to be in the drop zone.

He sat down as the toilet automatically flushed, misting the seat of his pants.

"Do you have the tapes?" the man to his right asked through a crack in the stall. The southern drawl in his voice was slight but noticeably there. This was the kidnapper he'd talked to on the phone.

"Is this restroom secure?" Jimmie asked.

"Our people did a sweep of it earlier," the woman to his left said. "We have someone standing guard out front. We're not going to be disturbed. We can talk freely."

"Before we start talking, I need to know who I'm dealing with," Jimmie said. "You know who I am. It only seems fair that I know your names."

"You didn't follow our directions," the man said. "I told you to put a fern out on your deck."

"That's what I did."

"It was a Ficus," the man said.

"Fern . . . Ficus . . . what does it matter?" Jimmie asked.

"You're not good at following instructions," the woman said.

"And maybe you're not good at giving them," Jimmie retorted. "That's not all on me. Now give me your names, or I walk."

"I'm sorry we haven't been up-front about things," the woman said. "It was for your protection, as well as ours."

"I'm a big boy—I can take care of myself."

"Just letting you know what's at stake here," the woman said. "My name is Hillary . . . and the man in the other stall is Jeb! We're the ones who are going to make America great again—again."

CHAPTER 55

★ ★ ★ ★

THE DREAM OF THE NINETIES IS ALIVE

Jimmie couldn't believe it. He stood up on the toilet, nearly dunking his foot in the process. He poked his head over the stall divider. Hillary Clinton waved at him. She was wearing a pink sweat suit, a fanny pack, and dark sunglasses, but it was her all right. A diamond-encrusted Bernie bird brooch was pinned to her top.

Jimmie then peered into the first stall. A man who looked like a bad Xerox of George W. Bush smiled from underneath a blue cap that read MAKE AMERICA GREAT AGAIN (AGAIN). Neither of them was exactly being subtle.

Jimmie carefully stepped off the toilet seat. What were the Clintons and the Bushes doing working together? The Clintons and the Bushes were the Capulets and the Montagues of modern politics. Unless the Bush daughters and Chelsea pulled a three-way Romeo and Juliet, there was no way the two families were ever going to stand united. Trump had done the impossible.

"You're Socialist Justice Warriors," Jimmie said. He was stating the obvious, but he needed time to process this turn of events. The stall was spinning around him; he needed to catch his breath and think.

"Check out the big brain on Brad," Hillary said. Jimmie recognized it as a quote from *Pulp Fiction*. Unsurprisingly, Hillary was still living in the nineties.

"You're working with Bernie now?" Jimmie said.

"No one's seen Bernie Sanders in years," Hillary said. "We're the ones who have been funding the Socialist Justice Warriors."

"The Bernie bros said they'd never support you."

"They have no idea who's pulling their strings," Hillary said. "But don't feel bad for them: They're a bunch of idealists. Even if they got the 'change' they wanted, they'd still find something to whine about. Ah, to be young."

"We represent the true change America needs," Jeb! said. "It's time for the lifelong politicians to take our country back. We're tired of getting bossed around by these Washington outsiders and their small-government underreaches. Our country should be governed the way the founders intended—by a small handful of political dynasties."

"The Clintons and the Bushes," Jimmie said.

"This is bigger than our families," Hillary said. "We're talking about the Democrats and Republicans."

"So wait another two years for the next presidential election," Jimmie said.

"The United States may not be around in two years if we get drawn into this conflict with Great Britain. They fight dirty," Jeb! said.

Jimmie folded the brochure. "Your brother got us into that mess in Iraq, and we're still here. Deeper in debt and less respected around the world, but what else is new?"

"If you're expecting me to defend my brother, you don't know Jeb!"

Not many people do know Jeb!, Jimmie thought.

"What's done is done," Hillary said. "The conflict in the Middle East was a limited skirmish. Yes, it destabilized the region . . . but it didn't destabilize the world. Al Qaeda is wiped out, and ISIS has been contained. But war with the UK is another beast entirely."

"*Two* beasts. A lion and a unicorn," interjected Jeb! "Because they're on the coat of arms over there."

"Shut up, Jeb!"

"Sorry."

Hillary continued, "My point is, France took our side in the Revolutionary War. Whose side will they take this time, especially after Trump's call to resculpt the Statue of Liberty so she shows more leg? Russia, on the other hand, will have Trump's back. Especially after he let Putin fight to a hero's death against that panda. That will put America at odds with almost every country we currently call allies. The entire geopolitical map is about to be redrawn, Mr. Bernwood."

"Unless you take Trump down," Jimmie said.

"Unless we take his entire administration down," Jeb! said. "They're corrupt from top to bottom. We'll need to clean house—starting with the man in charge."

"Tom Brady is next in line," Jimmie said.

"The vice president is in outer space," Hillary said. "You can't govern from outer space. It's in the Constitution."

"The speaker of the house will be sworn in," Jeb! said. "Ryan is a party guy."

"He likes to party, does he?" Jimmie asked.

"He's a card-carrying Republican," Hillary said.

"I was making a joke," Jimmie said.

"I don't know what those are," Hillary said.

So the Socialist Justice Warriors wanted what was best for America? Jimmie wasn't buying it. Hillary and Jeb!'s pitch to him to "save the country" came off as sour grapes. They'd both had their chance against Trump. The American people had spoken—loud and clear. In record numbers. The people trusted Trump to make the right decisions for their country. If you listened to polls, most of them were happy with their choice. Who was Jimmie to argue with them? While the Socialist Justice Warriors spoke about Trump as if he were a dictator, they were the ones trying to force themselves down America's throat. They were the ones attempting to dismantle the democracy.

No wonder Jimmie fucking hated politics.

"You don't have a mole in the White House, then?" Jimmie asked, fishing around to see if Christie was part of their organization.

"If we did, we wouldn't have had to kidnap your girlfriend," Hillary said. "Since you refused to assist the Socialist Justice Warriors, we've had to resort to . . . unsavory tactics. You left us no choice."

Hillary had known what she was doing when she called Cat his "girlfriend." He thought about disputing the taunt, but keeping his emotions in check was something he'd just picked up from Trump's book.

"Set the tapes on the ground and scoot them over," Hillary demanded.

Jimmie felt the recorder in his jacket pocket but didn't remove it. "Where's Cat?"

"She's safe," Jeb! said. "Just give us the damn tapes. Time is running out."

"Tell me where she is, or I drop the tapes into the toilet."

"You wouldn't," Jeb! said. "You wouldn't dare. You know how valuable—"

"He's bluffing," Hillary said. "He probably doesn't even have them on him."

Jimmie pressed PLAY on the recorder. Trump's voice echoed in the stall: *Here's what you do. You finance a boat, then you buy the boat company and run it into the ground. They close up shop, boom—free boat.*

He paused it.

"God dammit," Jeb! cried, pounding weakly on the divider. "Don't do it."

"He has duplicates somewhere," Hillary said, unfazed.

"I couldn't risk making a copy," Jimmie said. "The interview sessions are on a hard drive inside this recorder. No tapes. No copies. This is it."

According to *Trump: The Art of the Deal*, "the worst thing you can possibly do in a deal is seem desperate to make it. That makes the other guy smell blood, and then you're dead." Right now, Jeb! Bush was sweating desperation. Hillary was playing it cool. Jimmie wondered if she'd colored Trump's book.

"Your girlfriend is tied up in the *Taken* exhibit," Hillary said.

That was all Jimmie wanted to know. That was all he *needed* to know.

He unlocked the door.

"You think you're just going to walk out of here without handing over the device?" Hillary said. "Even if you get past both of our men at the restroom door, you'll never make it out of the museum alive. And neither will your girlfriend."

"You'll get the recorder as soon as I make sure she's safe," Jimmie said. "I'm in charge now. I'm the goddamn man. I'm—"

The overhead lights went out. This wasn't an uncommon occurrence in Trump's United States. You just sort of had to expect the rolling brownouts, as all caps on energy consumption had been lifted. Usually, the backup generators in most buildings kicked in after ten or fifteen seconds. Life would return to normal.

But this time, the darkness did not abate. Really? Did this have to happen right in the middle of his big speech where he turned the tables on the kidnappers?

A loud bang outside of the restroom startled Jimmie. It was quickly followed by another, and another. Gunshots.

CHAPTER FIFTY-SIX

★ ★ ★ ★

KILLING EVERYBODY

"**D**id you double-cross us, Jimmie?" Hillary asked in the darkness.

"How could I double-cross you? We were never on the same page to begin with."

Something landed on the floor outside the stalls with a metallic clang and started hissing like a snake. The room quickly filled with smoke. Jimmie covered his mouth with his T-shirt and crept up onto the toilet seat, where he crouched like Spider-Man.

A red laser cut through the darkness and danced above the stall door. The tiny shaft of light would have only been a red dot if not for the smoke clouding the air. Perched like he was on the toilet, Jimmie Bernwood was a shitting duck.

The red shaft of light passed under the stalls, bouncing off the shoes of his stallmates. He closed his eyes as it passed over the bare tile in front of his toilet. The gunshots outside indicated to him that somebody had taken out the Socialist Justice Warriors standing guard . . . but that didn't necessarily mean whoever was doing the shooting was after Hillary and Jeb! More likely, they were after the same thing everyone else seemed to be interested in: the Dorset recordings. And Jimmie didn't need to be alive to hand them over.

He opened his eyes just as gunfire erupted outside of the stalls. In such close quarters, it was loud enough to take what was left of Jimmie's hearing and leave a ringing in its place. After the first few rapid-fire shots, he stopped hearing them. The shooting was still going on, though, because the flashes of the muzzles were lighting up the restroom. It was as if somebody were throwing a Fourth of July fireworks show just for his private amusement. Some real asshole.

Jimmie braced for the bullets to enter his body and deliver him to the Lord. Although he'd always been an atheist, he prayed to God that the assassins left enough of him for at least a partially open casket. Those closed-casket affairs were just depressing as all shit—you always wondered just how mangled the corpse was beneath the pine lid.

Finally, the light show stopped.

Jimmie ran a hand over his chest and stomach, checking for wounds. Not a bullet hole to be found. He thanked God for saving him and went back to being an atheist.

The ringing in his ears slowly wound down, and he could make out a couple of voices arguing on the other side of the stall door. The lights flickered back on. Jimmie glanced down to see how his stallmates had fared, then quickly looked away. The floor was a mess of busted ceramic from the toilet seats, plaster chunks from the walls . . . and blood. So much blood. One of Jeb!'s loafers had somehow found its way back into Jimmie's stall. Part of a foot was still stuck in it, but it had come undone from the rest of Jeb!'s body.

There were footsteps across the broken tile outside Jimmie's stall. Then a pause. He could sense somebody standing there, contemplating his fate. An assassin. Jimmie decided to go down swinging.

"You'll never take me alive," he said, gripping the only weapon he had—the recorder—with both hands. His voice was trembling and weak.

The words had sounded so much better in his head.

CHAPTER FIFTY-SEVEN

✯ ✯ ✯ ✯

HIGH SCORE: 1,072

"If I show up with your casket in tow, the president will probably revoke my Medal of Honor," the man outside the stall said. His voice was like gravel. "But it's your choice, amigo. I get paid by the pound."

"The president?" Jimmie said. "You mean President Trump?"

"Goddamn right I mean President Trump. He's our boss—the commander in chief. And we have orders to bag your sorry ass. Open the door."

Jimmie unlocked the door and opened it a crack. The man he was talking to was dressed in camo from head to toe. Jimmie recognized the soldier's rifle as an FN SCAR (Special Operations Forces Combat Assault Rifle, an acronym he knew from his days playing the original *Human Hiroshima* on Xbox—er, his roommate's days of playing video games).

"Who's 'we'?" Jimmie asked.

"You're James Bernwood?" the soldier asked, ignoring his question.

Jimmie eyed the man's hands cradling the rifle. He nodded in the affirmative.

"I'm Sergeant Spencer Paul," the soldier said. "And we're SEAL Team Sixty-Nine."

"*The* Spencer Paul?" Jimmie asked. "The Human Hiroshima?"

"If you're asking if I'm the Spencer Paul who personally shot and killed one thousand seventy-two enemy combatants—the most confirmed kills in US military history—and who was the subject of the Bill O'Reilly book *Killing Everybody*, then yes."

Jimmie heard more footsteps. Three figures trotted from the fog to form a semicircle around Jimmie's stall with the celebrated Navy SEAL. "The perimeter is secure, sir," one of the other soldiers, a tough-as-buffalo-jerky-sounding woman, said. "Is this the baggage?"

"Baggage confirmed," Paul said, nodding.

Jimmie stepped out of the stall. The restroom was torn apart. It reminded him of his off-campus apartment senior year.

Immediately, all four soldiers pointed their weapons at Jimmie. A wet, warm feeling spread underneath his butt. He may have pissed himself. It wouldn't have been the first time, but it would have been the first time he'd done so while sober.

"What's that in your hand?" Paul shouted.

Jimmie raised his hands. "It's just a recording—"

"Set it on the ground."

He set it on the floor so that they could inspect it. Paul fired a single shot through it, causing Jimmie's heart to skip a beat. While it was practically worthless, it was all Jimmie had.

"Let's secure the LZ and get the hell out of here," Paul said.

"There's a woman being held captive," Jimmie said. "On the third floor, I think."

Paul nodded to the other soldiers, who filed out of the restroom. Paul waited behind with Jimmie, who wondered if kills on US soil counted toward Spencer Paul's astounding total. Probably not, he guessed.

Still, what had happened here today wasn't going to be swept under a rug. Covering up an apparent murder at the White House was one thing; covering up the brutal assassination of two former presidential candidates—one of whom, as the first lady, was supposed to still be under Secret Service protection— was beyond comprehension.

Jimmie had been wrong when he thought Trump was untouchable as far as scandal went. This had all happened in the middle of the day. With families around, even. And according to Spencer Paul, the order for the assault had come directly from the president himself.

Trump's political career was over. The recorder (or what was left of it) lying on the tile hardly mattered now, if it ever did in the first place.

A cheer erupted from outside in the hallway, and President Trump entered the restroom. It seemed that his political career wasn't over quite yet.

CHAPTER FIFTY-EIGHT

★ ★ ★ ★

DENY EVERYTHING

Spencer Paul saluted the commander in chief, who returned with an awkward wave of the hand. Trump still hadn't quite gotten the hang of being a politician. He was constantly fist-bumping hands raised for high fives and slapping babies instead of kissing them. The whole "politicians kissing babies" thing had never sat right with Jimmie, though, so he forgave Trump for that one.

Trump peeked into the stalls and frowned. "Jesus, you SEALs don't play around."

"No, sir, we do not," Paul said.

"Christie's on his way over here to clean this up," Trump said. Then, to Jimmie, he added, "The country thanks you for your help unveiling the plot against the presidency. Shame it had to go down like this on a perfectly fine holiday weekend, but I suppose cutting my trip to Mar-a-Lago short was worth it to extinguish a domestic terror threat. As I'm sure you understand, Jimmie, we'll need to keep all of this top secret. Not a word to anyone—even your mother."

"My mother's dead."

"Then that should make it easy not to tell her."

"Did they find Cat?" Jimmie blurted.

"The reporter?" Trump said. He looked to Paul, who radioed the other SEALs for an update.

"The baggage has been located," the celebrity SEAL said. "We're taking her to the nearest hospital as a precaution. She's in shock, but she otherwise appears to be unharmed."

Jimmie was glad to hear that. He wished the SEALs would stop referring to people they rescued as "baggage," but it was probably a better term than what they called them when they weren't in the room.

"What about the people out there?" Jimmie said. "There was a military operation on American soil. In broad daylight. People had to have taken pictures. They had to have heard the gunshots—"

"All part of a demonstration at the International Spy Museum," Trump said. "As far as any of the turdfaces know, there were no live rounds fired during the exhibition. They do interactive stuff like this all the time around here. The kids love it."

Trump stumbled over the broken recorder and kicked it out of the way. He seemed rather pleased with the mayhem. "And if anyone finds out what really happened . . . I signed an executive order last night classifying these SJW clowns as domestic terrorists. I'm keeping America safe."

You're keeping you *safe*, Jimmie thought.

Instead of saying what was on his mind, though, he said, "Emma was murdered last night."

"I heard. You did an excellent job with the plumbing work," Trump said. "When I told you we had a leak, I had no idea you would find it so quickly. Can't believe she slipped under my radar. That's what a nice set of gams will do to a guy! England almost had us by the balls there. And today—well, you've certainly gone above and beyond my expectations, Jimmie. Rooting out a spy *and* leading these blue-cap-wearing bozos straight to us? You deserve a reward."

Trump pulled out a business card. "Use this at the Watergate hotel spa for fifteen percent off anything," the president said. "My treat."

Trump took a step, then turned back to Jimmie. "Stick with me, kid, and you'll go places. Just saying, there's going to be an opening soon for governor of Wales. Think about it."

Trump slapped Spencer Paul on the back, and the two men walked out together, laughing. Jimmie shook his head and dropped the card.

Trump was coming unhinged—if he'd ever been hinged in the first place. Putin's death hadn't tamed his bravado. Congress was going to come around any day now. With the leaders of the resistance movement and who knew how many of their foot soldiers out of the way, there was no one standing between the president and his insane thirst for war with the United Kingdom.

No one but Jimmie Bernwood.

Bill Clinton burst into the restroom with a flurry of energy. "You guys need to check out this shirt I got at the gift . . . shop . . ." His voice trailed off as he surveyed the destruction, wide-eyed. The shirt he was wearing read "DENY EVERYTHING."

"I'm sorry, Mr. President," Jimmie said. "Your wife . . ."

Bill caught his breath and poked his head into the stall where Hillary lay. Or what was left of her. He turned quickly away from the gruesome scene. A single tear streaked down his rosy cheek. Bill pulled Jimmie in for a hug. They'd never met before, but how could you say no to a grieving man?

"Hug your loved ones tonight," Bill said. "Life is precious."

Jimmie promised him he would.

Bill wiped the tear away. "Say, do you know how late that Bond girls exhibit is open upstairs?"

CHAPTER FIFTY-NINE

★ ★ ★ ★

TO CATCH A RAT

On Jimmie's way out of the museum, he saw Cat being helped into the back of an ambulance. She brushed the paramedics away and gave Jimmie a quick hug.

"What the hell did you get us into?" she whispered, thankfully ignoring his wet pants. "You said this had to do with Lester, and then I'm kidnapped by a bunch of activists wearing Cubs hats, and they're telling me you have some tapes . . . ?"

His eyes darted from rooftop to rooftop. He knew that he was on thin ice—that this thing wasn't over. While the president pretended that Jimmie had "led them" to Emma and the SJWs, they both knew that was a lie. If he said the wrong thing, was the *Killing Everybody* hero standing by to take him out?

"I don't have the tapes," he told Cat.

"What?" she said.

"They were destroyed in the shootout."

"You made copies, though."

He shook his head.

Her eyes widened. "So this was all for nothing—is that what you're saying?"

"It's not for nothing. I saved you."

"The SEALs saved me."

He said, "Well, I was just *about* to save you, when SEAL Team Sixty-Nine kicked in the door and started blowing holes in everything. I wish I'd had the tapes still, but your life is what's important."

"Why did you get me involved in this?"

"I thought you'd want to know what happened to Lester. I thought you'd want some closure," he said.

"Bullshit. There was something in it for you. Let me guess: You needed somewhere to publish whatever was on that recorder's hard drive, right? And now it's gone forever because you were too stupid to make a copy."

"You're calling *me* stupid? You—"

He paused. He'd never mentioned the recorder to her. The SJWs hadn't known it was a recorder either—everyone thought the interviews were recorded on cassette tapes. The only ones who knew about the recorder other than Jimmie and the Trumps were Lester and Emma . . . and Lester and Emma were both dead. Had the president enlisted Cat to suss out leaks too? Was he just playing them against each other?

"You . . . you're right," Jimmie said. "I'm stupid. A big dummy."

Cat folded her arms. "You finally admit it. Now are you going to explain what's going on? Give me a clue. You said this had to do with Lester . . ."

He decided to gamble.

"I know who killed him."

She was silent for a moment. Then she said, "He killed himself."

Jackpot. For somebody who hadn't known her ex-boyfriend was even dead, she seemed to have a very specific idea of how he died. And a very *suspicious* specific idea, at that.

Suddenly, Jimmie's whole world seemed to be crashing down around him. Lewandowski wasn't the last of the suspects in Lester's murder—Cat had just added herself to Jimmie's list. He couldn't believe how blind he'd been. He'd been so focused on those who'd had rooftop access that he'd overlooked the obvious: The killer didn't need a badge. Not if Lester had taken them up there. Was Cat the shadow he'd been searching for?

"I'll explain everything," Jimmie said, loud and clear enough for snooping ears to pick up. "But not here. It's not safe. Meet me tomorrow night at nine. The Lincoln Memorial."

"Right out in the open. How is that any safer than on a street corner? Maybe we should meet somewhere more out of the way. Like . . . your room at the Watergate?"

She gazed up at him. Even after an eighteen-hour kidnapping ordeal, she could still mesmerize him with those big, bold eyes. This time, however, he wasn't buying what she was selling.

"It's been compromised," Jimmie said. "See you tomorrow. Oh, and another thing? Try to be a doll and not get kidnapped this time."

She swung a hand at him, but he grabbed her wrist before she could slap him across the face.

"Still an asshole," she muttered, struggling free.

To the casual observer, Jimmie's comment about getting kidnapped would have sounded like an impossibly cruel thing to say. But he'd said it to provoke a reaction out of her, and damned if she hadn't responded as expected.

Besides, Jimmie wasn't expecting casual observers to overhear him. He was expecting trained ears to be listening in to their conversation. Not only was he expecting it, but he was counting on it. Sometimes, to catch a rat, you had to use a Cat as bait.

CHAPTER SIXTY

★ ★ ★ ★

LUCIFER IN THE FLESH

"You really sure you want to do this?" Darrell Riley asked. The six-foot-six man with the Texas drawl was the warden at the Pit, a for-profit, maximum-security prison on a sprawling patch of land in Dulles County, Virginia.

"I wouldn't be here if I didn't have to be," Jimmie Bernwood said.

"Shit, I wouldn't be either," Riley said, holding his palm up to a security sensor.

A door straight out of *Star Trek* opened for them, and they entered the Pit's solitary confinement wing.

Jimmie's visitor badge identified him as "Barry Oliver." An FBI agent. He'd called in some old favors—the last favors he had in his debit account—and set up an appointment Sunday morning to see one of the prison's highest-profile prisoners. Jimmie was already waist-deep in shit . . . why not dunk his head all the way under?

"You really think this guy has any information on your killer?" Riley asked as they walked down a long, barren corridor.

"Doubtful."

Riley screeched to a halt. "Then why are we down here on a Sunday morning? I could be at church right now."

"And I could be tailgating in the parking lot at the Washington Palefaces game," Jimmie said. "It's still the preseason, but at least the beer's real even if the football ain't. Unfortunately, another body turned up last night along the turnpike. Same markings as before. Second one this month."

"I haven't heard about any of this on the news."

That's because none of it is true, you nincompoop.

"We've managed to keep it out of the news," Jimmie said. "People would freak out if they knew somebody was out there re-creating the Zodiac killings right down to the last detail."

Two armed guards stood alert outside the cell door and backed away to give Riley room to use his palm to gain access. The security here was tighter than at the White House.

Jimmie flipped absentmindedly through his file folder, which was stuffed with printouts of the original Zodiac killing victims.

"He may not have information about this new killer, but we believe he's the only one who can help us get in the mind of the killer," Jimmie said.

The door slid open. A long walkway led directly to a glass cage measuring twenty feet on all sides. The shirtless prisoner was facing away in the other direction, but Jimmie could see that his upper body was bursting with tattooed muscle. There was a mattress on the floor of the cage and a bedpan, but nothing else. It reminded Jimmie of the time he'd caught a praying mantis as a kid. He'd placed the insect inside an old fishbowl with a few blades of grass. It had died after three days.

"There he is," Riley said. "Rafael Edward Cruz. 'Ted,' to his friends—if you can find any."

Jimmie laughed, because he thought that was what the warden expected of him.

"There's nothing funny about a man who's killed as many innocent people as Cruz has," Riley snapped.

"Sorry, you work with sick sons of bitches day in, day out, you tend to get a twisted sense of humor, you know what I mean?"

Riley shook his head. "Just get on with it so we can both get home before the game starts."

Jimmie started toward the cage. The pathway wasn't simply a pathway—it was a bridge. On either side, it dropped off into an infinite darkness. So this was why they called it the Pit. Somewhere in the building, he guessed there was also a pendulum. Edgar Allan Poe had once lived in Virginia, so it made sense. In an insane way.

He stopped. Riley wasn't following him. "You're not coming?"

"This is as close as I get to that monster," the warden shouted from the doorway. "I'll be right on the other side of the door. If you need help . . . shout. Not that it will do you any good."

"He can't get out, can he?"

"Theoretically, no. But they also said he couldn't be the Zodiac Killer because he was born two years after the killings began—and look how wrong they were."

Jimmie nodded. Before he reached the glass cage, he heard the door close behind him. He was all alone with the man authorities believed to be one of the most prolific and vicious serial killers in history. The man whose presidential aspirations Jimmie had personally destroyed with a two-hour-plus sex tape. The man who had every reason in the world to want revenge on him. Would several inches of industrial-strength glass be enough to hold Ted Cruz back?

"Mr. Bernwood," Cruz said without turning around. "What an unpleasant surprise." And his thin, ghoulish giggling filled the room.

CHAPTER SIXTY-ONE

★ ★ ★ ★

AS BIG AS IT GETS

"**Y**ou must have me confused with somebody else," Jimmie said, standing close to the glass. The smell of sulfur drifted through the tiny holes drilled at intervals along the glass wall. "I'm Larry Oliver, with the Federal Bureau of Investigation—"

"Your badge says *Barry* Oliver," Cruz said, still facing away from him.

"'Larry' is short for 'Barry,'" Jimmie said.

"Drop the act. You may have fooled the warden, but you haven't fooled everybody at this facility. You wouldn't have made it this far unless I let you. I've had the cameras turned off for the occasion. Nobody's watching . . ."

Which meant that nobody could save Jimmie should Cruz attack him. He took a step back from the glass.

"I never got a chance to thank you, Mr. Bernwood."

"Thank me?"

"Oh, did I say thank you? I meant *kill* you. I never got a chance to *kill* you."

"I'm not here to dredge up old grudges," Jimmie said.

Cruz spun around and with lightning quickness was at the glass. "I get to say when the hatchet is buried," he hissed. "Not you."

Up close, Cruz was less Grandpa Munster and more Grandpa Monster. Prison had hardened him almost beyond recognition.

The prison tattoos covering his body told a tale—the tale of a man who'd gone off the deep end. LUCIFER was writ large in gangsta lettering across his chiseled abs; SAM I AM wrapped around his neck. Perhaps more worrying, however, was how prison had reshaped his face. The lines around his eyes were deep and pronounced. He looked like he hadn't slept since they'd thrown him in this cage—either because they never turned the overhead lights off or because he was just that stone-cold of a badass now.

"I need your help," Jimmie said.

"There is no copycat killer, is there?" Cruz said. "What's the real reason you're here?"

"It has to do with Trump."

The color drained from Cruz's face.

"That's right," Jimmie said. "The man who put you in this hellhole. You remember Trump?"

Cruz clawed at his ears. "Stop saying that name! Stop saying that name!"

"It was Trump who did this to you, not me. Trump."

Cruz banged a fist on the glass.

Jimmie stood his ground.

"You might have been able to get back in the race if not for the sex-tape scandal," Jimmie said. "People expected you to stick around until the bitter end. They liked you *because* you were spiteful and delusional. Who knows? If that tape hadn't come out, you might even have beaten him on the second or third ballot at the convention. Not necessarily—anything can happen in American politics, or so I've been told—but you had a chance. Instead, someone in his camp leaked it, and . . . you know the rest."

Cruz crumpled to the ground. He curled into a ball, shaking and making a sound like a whoopee cushion with asthma.

Jimmie pushed on. "I'm sorry about the role I played in it, but now I need your help. The country needs your help."

"They framed me," Cruz said between sobs.

"I know. There's no way you could have committed the Zodiac killings."

"*Trump* framed me."

"That's right," Jimmie said. "*President Trump* framed you."

Ted Cruz got to his feet. He wiped the tears from his cheeks. "What do you need from me? An interview for a story?"

Jimmie shook his head. "This is bigger than just a story," he said, opening the file and removing the paper clip from the printouts. "This is as big as it gets."

As Jimmie explained to Cruz what he would need him to do, the convicted murderer's eyes grew wider, and giggles escaped his throat at odd intervals. The man was clearly delirious. At various points, Jimmie could almost see Ted Cruz as a serial-killing lunatic.

Good. For what Jimmie needed him for, he'd have to play the part. For what Jimmie needed him for, Ted Cruz was going to have to be the killer the world thought that he was.

☆ ☆ ☆ ☆

Excerpt From the Trump/Dorset Sessions

July 2, 2018, 3:36 PM

DORSET: You're a big proponent of the Second Amendment and the rights of gun owners in general. Are you carrying a firearm right now?

234

TRUMP: I have a concealed-carry permit, but if I were to answer your question in the negative, it might embolden my enemies. If I answer in the affirmative, it would probably piss off the Secret Service. It's a no-win. I'd rather keep everyone guessing. Let's just say I'm not happy to see you.

DORSET: Has the Secret Service told you not to carry a gun?

TRUMP: There's nothing in the Constitution forbidding the president from carrying a gun. I could carry a bazooka if I wanted to. But you know how people get—they think you're stepping on their toes. It's their job to protect the president. If I can defend myself, there goes their livelihood. They'd be more comfortable with a wimp like Obama.

DORSET: Can we talk about President Obama for a couple of minutes?

TRUMP: Two minutes. I'm not wasting more time than I have to on that clown.

DORSET: In 2011, you became the public face of the so-called birther movement. You questioned whether the president was actually born in the United States and thus eligible to be commander in chief. President Obama eventually released the long-form version of his Hawaiian birth certificate to quell the flames.

In the days and months that followed, did you ever regret raising the issue?

TRUMP: First off, I reject the term "birther." It's derogatory. It just sounds icky, like childbirth. And secondly, I'm still very proud of what I was able to accomplish. As a private citizen of the United States, I successfully petitioned the president. I did what no one else could do. The White House produced his birth certificate, which looked very realistic, I'll give them that. The media bought it, at least.

DORSET: You never did—one of your first acts as president was to revoke his US citizenship. You deported him and his family to Hawaii.

TRUMP: That's correct.

DORSET: You do know that Hawaii is within the United States, right?

TRUMP: Your hundred and twenty seconds are up.

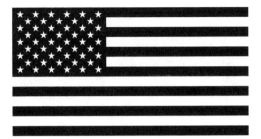

Sunday, September 2, 2018

CHAPTER SIXTY-TWO

⭐ ⭐ ⭐ ⭐

THE SERIES FINALE

Jimmie had never seen the Lincoln Memorial at night before. The famous statue of Lincoln seated like Captain Picard in his captain's chair was brilliantly lit from all sides. The stone columns supporting the ceiling cast majestic shadows across the wide cement staircase where Jimmie stood. He'd chosen to meet Cat here because it was the one place in the city Trump hadn't fingered with his Midas touch. Lincoln was the lone president that Trump was on record as admiring—because, as Trump once said, "He's the greatest vampire hunter our country has ever seen."

But Jimmie wasn't here to admire the unmolested monument. If everything went according to plan, there'd be time for admiration later.

"Where is everybody?" Cat asked, approaching from the south. She was walking with purpose. She wanted to get this over with as fast as possible.

That made two of them.

Jimmie rose to greet her. "It's nine o'clock on the Sunday night before Labor Day," he said. "They're all at home watching the *Game of Thrones* series finale. Even G. R. R. Martin is watching to see how it ends."

"I never understood that fantasy shit," Cat said, keeping a few feet between them. That was fine by Jimmie—he had no interest in being smacked again or thrown to the ground.

"I don't watch it either. I'm still on season two of *The Wire*," he said. "I'm, like, five premium cable series behind."

His choice of date and time had been deliberate. Once night had fallen, the Memorial and the adjoining National Mall had cleared out. An eerie calm had come over DC . . . an eerie calm that would soon be shattered.

"You said you know who killed Lester," Cat said. "But that's impossible. He committed suicide. He jumped off the roof of the White House. His body was found in the Rose Garden."

"You said before that his death was news to you," Jimmie said.

"I didn't know if I could trust you."

"So why didn't you write about his death, then?" Jimmie said.

"You know as well as I do that this is a click-driven business."

"So you didn't even investigate it? He was your boyfriend."

"*Was* my boyfriend. Remember that I'm a member of the White House press corps. I'm not paid to investigate," Cat said. "Besides, 'Old-School News Reporter Kills Self at White House' isn't exactly going to garner many views."

"Let the people make that decision," Jimmie said.

She shook her head. "The people *did* decide—years and years ago. Before the advent of blogging, before the advent of the Internet. There's maybe some political intrigue there. *Maybe*. But it's miniscule. Bottom line is reporters aren't celebrities. Nobody cares when they drop dead." Cat pulled a snub-nosed revolver from her handbag. "That's why nobody's going to care when you're found facedown in the Reflecting Pool, drowned."

CHAPTER SIXTY-THREE

✬ ✬ ✬ ✬

THINK OF THE PAGEVIEWS!

Jimmie sighed. "I hoped I was wrong about you."

"How does it feel being right about me?"

"Like a kick to Little Jimmie," he said.

"We can arrange that. Now get moving," she said, waving the gun toward the pond. "What tipped you off?"

"You mean, when did I first suspect you had a hidden agenda?" Jimmie said. "You slipped up a few times when we were talking outside the museum. When you tried to slap me and I grabbed your wrist, however, I knew for sure. You didn't have any rope marks or handcuff imprints."

"Maybe they weren't tied very tight."

"I thought about that, but you'd have at least struggled. You put up a fight the other day when I just tried to say hello," Jimmie said. "So we know you didn't struggle. My first thought was that you orchestrated the kidnapping. But using Occam's razor, the simplest answer is usually correct. You *were* kidnapped, but you didn't struggle. Why was that?"

"I suppose you have an answer for that," she said, prodding him down the steps.

"I do," he said. "Trump used you as bait—bait for the Socialist Justice Warriors to make a move. I'm guessing that some time ago, you noticed one of their hackers had found a back door into your phone. That's how they knew where you were going to be last Friday night; that's why you accepted my invitation to dinner. That's why you had to set it up a few days in advance—to surreptitiously give them a heads-up."

"I'm surprised you didn't suspect something was up when I agreed to go on a date with you. Men. You all think with your dicks."

Jimmie swung around. "It wasn't a date. Was it?"

Cat leveled the gun at him. "Keep. Walking."

"Or what, you're going to shoot me?"

"I'm seriously considering it," she said. "The idea is becoming more attractive by the minute. Now move."

She prodded him with the tip of the pistol. Even though it was a small, snub-nosed handgun like you'd see a dame carrying in an old noir movie, it could probably poke a hole or two in him if she pulled the trigger.

"You killed Lester, didn't you?" Jimmie said. "It wasn't Lewandowski. It was you."

"Is this supposed to be the scene in the little suspense novel running through your head where the villain explains herself? Sorry to disappoint you or your nonexistent readers, Jimmie, but if you don't know by now, you're too shitty of a detective to live."

"You're not denying you killed him."

"Trying to get me to implicate myself again?" she said. "I might as well tell you, if only because I think you'd understand why I did it. I lied about the last time I saw Lester alive. It wasn't in June—it was in July. It had been a few months since we'd split. We saw each other in passing a few days before the Fourth of July, and he asked if I wanted to watch the fireworks from the roof of the White House. Of course, he just wanted to get back together, but how do you say no to that?"

They reached the edge of the Reflecting Pool. In the water, Jimmie could see President Lincoln staring out over Cat's shoulder. The gun was at Jimmie's back.

"Wade into the pond," Cat said.

"Can I take my shoes and socks off first? If I were going to drown naturally, you know, that's what I would do. You want this to look realistic, I assume."

She sighed and motioned for him to hurry up. As he stripped his shoes and socks off, she continued her story.

"At quarter 'til nine, we went up to the roof using his orange-level clearance. I guess because he wanted to impress me, he let it slip that he had some 'explosive' recordings of things the president had said to him. Due to his nondisclosure agreement, he couldn't publish them. Or he was too scared to. He was thinking about handing the recordings off to some of his liberal pals. Just handing them over to a bunch of Bernie bros!"

"What a waste," Jimmie said. He wasn't ready yet to mention the recordings were worthless. He dipped a toe into the water, and it sent a chill up his spine. Though the weather had been in the sixties all week and was probably there right now, the water felt much, much colder.

"Exactly—that's what I said. Think of the pageviews! He had hours and hours of this stuff, with the president on tape saying the most outrageous stuff. To use Trump's own terminology, it was a gold mine."

Jimmie stepped into the pool. The water came halfway up his shins. Goose bumps rose all over his body.

Cat said, "Lester said he'd hidden the recorder within the White House. Somewhere in his office was my guess. He wouldn't listen to reason, though. I did the only thing I could do: I went for his badge. There was a struggle . . . and he went over the edge. I tried telling myself it was an accident . . . but I know it wasn't."

"You didn't get the badge, I'm guessing."

She shook her head. "He took it with him, right into the Rose Garden. After the Secret Service shot him to death, I got the hell out of there. I thought the recorder had been tossed or erased . . . until you showed up. I began to think there might be some hope—and, as it turns out, I was right. You know, that thing was my ticket out of this town. Then you went and fucked that all up. Not only that, but you cracked the case of Lester's death. I'm not ready to go to jail. Orange is not the new black. I look worse than Christie in orange."

At least he agreed with her there.

"Why kill me?" he asked.

"This is all your fault—all of this," she said. "If you hadn't posted that stupid Ted Cruz sex tape without my approval, neither of us would be in this mess right now."

"I thought you'd be impressed by it."

"Impressed that someone leaked you a tape? You were the only journalist with low enough scruples to post something that . . . disgusting."

"I thought it would win a Pulitzer."

"A Pulitzer?" she said. "This is about Lester, isn't it?"

"Not entirely. But—"

"I didn't leave you for Lester because he had a Pulitzer Prize," she said. "I left you for him because he wasn't so insecure."

Okay, that hurt. Jimmie inched his way across the cement floor of the pool. If she was going to kill him, why did she have to be so mean about it?

"How far do you want me to go, your highness?" he said.

There was no answer from behind him.

He turned his head.

Ted Cruz was standing at the edge of the pool, his chiseled body illuminated by the moonlight. He had an arm around Cat's neck. She'd gone limp.

"Jesus, don't kill her!" Jimmie said, sloshing his way back to the grass.

A gunshot rang out across the yard, and Cruz and Cat both fell into a heap. Jimmie swung around, looking for the assailant. Could be the Human Hiroshima; could be an assassin from any number of government organizations.

He felt a thump on the back of his head, and everything went black.

CHAPTER SIXTY-FOUR

★ ★ ★ ★

NO SPOILERS

When Jimmie came to, he found himself tied to a pillar facing Lincoln. The thick rope wrapped around him several times, pinning his arms to his sides. There was a pounding sensation in the back of his skull where he'd been hit.

Although his vision was slightly blurred from being knocked out, he could make out two other figures tied up in a similar fashion—to his left, Ted Cruz, who was bleeding profusely from a wound in his shoulder. To Jimmie's right, Cat Diaz. She was still unconscious.

"Wish somebody could sing the national anthem right now," a familiar voice said. Trump. "Wouldn't that be something?"

"Ooooh saaaay can you seeeeeee, by the Donald's early light—"

"Can it, Christie."

Jimmie could hear Trump marching triumphantly up the steps, each footfall echoing through the stone corridors of the great monument. Finally, Trump came within view of Jimmie. The president was dressed the same as always, in a dark-navy suit and Day-Glo-red power tie. Chris Christie trailed him, wearing a scuba-diving suit. Had he been hiding in the Reflecting Pool? Trump's press secretary, Corey Lewandowski, brought up the rear. He was carrying an AR-15 with a steak knife duct-taped to the end like a bayonet. The gun should have blown a hole the size of a softball through Cruz's shoulder, but the bullet must have had a difficult time digging through all that muscle he'd put on doing push-ups in the Pit.

Trump examined Cruz, who snarled at him and gnashed his teeth.

"Somebody needs to go back in their cage," the president said before moving on. He stopped in front of Jimmie. "And you . . . I had such high hopes for you."

"That's kind of what I do—disappoint people."

"You were supposed to be my eyes and ears. I never asked you to be my dick."

"The first lady—"

"Shut it," Trump said. "She told me everything."

The president and pals moved on to Cat, who still hadn't shown any signs of life. "And you . . . where do I even start?"

Trump shook his head and returned his attention to Jimmie. "You thought you were being all smart, didn't you? Slipping that paper clip to Ted in his cell, which allowed him to escape this afternoon. When I got the surveillance photos of you being checked in, I said, 'No friggin' way is Jimmie Bernwood that dumb.' But here you are. Not feeling so smart now, are you?"

Jimmie didn't answer.

"That's okay, don't say anything," Trump said. "Even though you helped spring Ted from the joint, I bet you still don't have any idea who leaked you that sex tape of his, do you?"

Jimmie had thought about it briefly when he'd received the DVD in the mail, but the package had been sent anonymously. No return address, except for an obviously fake name ("John

Miller"). No one ever claimed ownership of it—which was just as well, because it had allowed him to state in court that he truthfully had no idea who sent it. But c'mon. If not Trump himself, it was *someone* in Trump's camp.

Trump turned to Cruz, who was struggling to stay conscious. "It's time to stop lying, Lying Ted. Care to tell Jimmie the truth?"

"I did it," Cruz said.

Trump grinned from ear to ear.

Jimmie stared incredulously at the tied-up former senator. Was it true? The more he thought about it, the more he knew it had to be. There was, after all, only one person in the sex tape: Ted Cruz. He'd filmed himself making love to an inflatable orca. He'd even supplied all of his "costar's" dialogue himself, speaking in a falsetto. Even though Cruz wore boxers throughout the entire film, it was easily one of the most disturbing things Jimmie had ever seen—and he'd seen every David Lynch film.

"Why'd you do it?" Jimmie asked.

"People kept mocking me," Cruz said. "They said mean, hateful things about me . . . that I was a serial killer, that I was an extraterrestrial wearing a human suit. I wanted voters to know I wasn't some weirdo. I put on music and taped myself having sex with an inflatable toy lady whale, just like your average Joe Six-Pack."

Jimmie shook his head. "Well, that seriously blew up in your face."

He immediately regretted his choice of words, as it echoed the final frames of the video where the orca popped and nearly suffocated Cruz. It was actually a scary moment, because at first Jimmie had thought he was watching a snuff film. It was a snuff film, in a way—for that poor orca. No wonder the jury had awarded SeaWorld such a large sum.

But Cruz's head was slumped down. The blood loss had finally gotten to him.

Trump returned to Jimmie. "Nine o'clock on Sunday night. *This* Sunday night. You prick."

"Somebody missing their dragons and tits?"

"If somebody spoils *Game of Thrones* for me before I have a chance to see it, I'm going to dig your body up and kill you again." Trump paused. "Oh, wait. I still have to kill you the first time, don't I?"

CHAPTER SIXTY-FIVE

★ ★ ★ ★

THE ONE WITH MEL GIBSON

"**W**here does it end?" Jimmie said.

Trump squinted. "Where does what end?"

"The trail of bodies . . . the thirst for power. Where does it all end?"

"I'll tell you where it ends," Trump said. "It ends with me on top of the world. I don't care if the world is a nuclear wasteland. You ever see *Mad Max?* Not the girl one, but the good one. The one with Mel Gibson. That's going to be me."

Jimmie wasn't buying it. "Cool story, bro."

"You don't think I have it in me?"

"You'd never let the world slip into chaos—all your money would be worthless. Anarchy is the enemy of the ruling class."

"Okay, you got me," Trump said. "You're learning a lot about politics. I'm almost impressed. *Almost.*"

The president pulled his gun out of his jacket holster. If the Secret Service were around, they would probably have flipped out. But Trump had apparently given them the slip. Even the Navy SEALs were absent. Only his top two henchmen had the pleasure of joining him on Mission: Clean Up the Loose Ends.

250

"Lester's recordings," Jimmie spat out.

Trump gave him a quizzical look.

"I made a backup of Lester's recordings," Jimmie said.

"Don't ever play poker," Trump said. "You've got a terrible poker face. Worst I've ever seen. And I've played against Anne Hathaway."

"Look me in my eyes and tell me I'm lying."

Trump narrowed his eyes at him. Dark-orange crevices formed on the president's brow. "Where's the backup?"

"Up my ass," Jimmie said with glee.

Trump slapped him. "Don't screw with me. Where is it?"

"On a Hello Kitty flash drive, up my butt. I'd need someone's help to get it out."

There was only one way for them to check whether or not he was lying, and that was to untie him from the pillar and give him an unlicensed prostate exam. Once they untied him, however, he'd find a way to slap the gun out of someone's hand. Then he'd save the goddamn day. Check. Mate.

"It's in your butt, huh?" Trump said. "Then you're going to be buried with it. That was easy."

Mission *not* accomplished.

"Not that it would matter," Trump said. "Haven't you figured it out by now? There's literally nothing I can say that will actually hurt me. It's just 'the Donald saying what he thinks.' It's just 'the Donald telling it like it is.' If you published them as a book, you'd hit number one on the *Times* best-seller list."

"Telling it like it is?" Jimmie said. "That's just another way of saying you call people names. You're just . . . being shitty."

Trump nodded. "I'll let you in on the secret: All these yahoos out there in flyover country don't *want* to be fat and poor with crappy jobs in towns with no live theatre. That's the hand they were dealt, and they're frustrated. Their lives are shitty, and they want to take it out on someone.

"Used to be, you could be shitty to the blacks. Then somebody said, *Oh, no, we can't be shitty to the blacks anymore.* Then we were shitty to Kardashians and somebody flipped out about that too. The real problem in this country is the PC police. Who do they think they are, trying to guilt-trip us over wanting to exercise our God-given American right to be shitty to people who are different than we are? It's been bottled up for too long—you can taste it in the air when it's released.

"So when people see me saying the stuff out loud that they can only scream at their TVs? I'm their hero. I'm living the new American dream, Jimmie: being an asshole and getting away with it. And if I can do it, maybe they can do it too."

Jimmie gaped at Trump. "That's crazy."

"No, the Republican establishment was crazy for ignoring such a huge sector of angry registered voters. Millions of pissed off, frustrated people just waiting to be mobilized. The other Republican candidates acted like they were too good for them. Not me, my friend. Know your market. Maximize your options. That's from the expanded edition of the number-one best-selling book of all time, *Trump: The Art of the Deal.*"

"I know," said Jimmie. "It took me six full boxes of crayons, but I finally made it through the damn thing."

"So you know the first rule: Think big. Did you ever stop to ask yourself why I chose Lester Dorset as my ghostwriter? Why would I invite one of my harshest critics into the White House?"

"To neuter him," Jimmie said.

"Wrong. I didn't want to neuter him—quite the contrary. When no one in the intelligence community could pin down the blue-cap threat, I decided to throw a little chum into the water.

"Dorset jumped at the chance to spend time with a sitting president. We gave him the same deal we gave you. He could follow me around and whatever, but he didn't seem as interested in that as in the interview sessions. The beauty of it was I just had to be myself in the interviews. I think he believed that 'the Donald' was this persona. A TV character. That in private, I'd tone things down. Instead, I put a little extra polish on my bon mots, just for him. You should have seen him! His eyes lit up like a kid on Christmas morning every time I said something that offended him. It was only a matter of time before he started telling his libtard friends about the killer quotes I was giving him. I just had to sit back and wait.

"After a couple of months, the sharks started circling. The Socialist Justice Warriors. Before we could reel them in, though, Kitty Cat over here throws our bait right off the goddamn roof! We should have just pinned Lester's death on her right then and there."

"Why didn't you?" Jimmie asked. "It would have been easy, especially if you had the surveillance video."

"Then we would have had to explain why the Secret Service shot him, and it would have opened a whole barrel of monkeys. No thanks. Christie thought it was best to forget about the whole thing. Hang onto what we knew for the time being, in case we needed to put pressure on the *Daily Blabber*. The bigger problem was that we couldn't find the recorder. I thought we'd have to start all the way over with you and string you along the same way to draw these social justice clowns in. I didn't count on you being so strangely . . . competent.

"I told Emma we should go for another *New York Times* liberal patsy, but she insisted you were a better choice. Now I know why—she was trying to undermine me. She wanted someone who wouldn't get involved in the politics. Someone who would stay in their lane. How wrong she was."

"So you didn't know she was a spy?"

"No idea! When I mentioned a 'leak,' I was just trying to make you dance a little. See if it wouldn't help stir up the resistance into making a move. Which Cat here was willing to assist with by acting as bait, once we let her know that *we* knew where she'd been that night with Lester. And I was right—I always am." The president pointed his gun at Jimmie's head. "But if you'll excuse me, I've got a show to watch. I hear tonight that the dragon chick is finally gonna bang Tyrion. Too bad you won't be alive to see it."

Jimmie closed his eyes. Before he could recant his atheism once more, he heard the clang of metal on the floor. He opened one eye. Christie had Trump in a bear hug from behind. The gun was lying on the floor at Trump's feet. Lewandowski was pounding away at Christie with the butt of his rifle, trying to get the former New Jersey governor to release the president. It was like watching the panda fight all over again.

Christie lowered a shoulder and twisted, rolling Trump onto the ground. Lewandowski fell forward, slamming the butt of his gun accidentally into Trump's face and impaling himself on the knife attached to the barrel.

The president uttered a string of expletives that would have gotten a lesser politician impeached. Christie slammed the president's head into the ground with his ginormous paw. Trump slumped over onto the lifeless body of his press secretary.

Christie pulled a switchblade from his pocket and sliced the ropes binding Jimmie in one swift motion.

"Why are you helping me?" Jimmie said. "I led the Socialist Justice Warriors right into Trump's tiny hands."

"You're a good guy," Christie said. "But you're dumb as shit. This was never about the Democrats or Republicans for me—or, God help me, the Clintons and Bushes. I deserved that VP slot, not that pretty-boy ball-licker. I was biding my time until the right dirt showed up on Trump. I don't know what's on these interview tapes, but if everybody wants it, it must be pretty important."

"There's nothing on them! Weren't you listening?" Jimmie said with a sigh. "Don't you get it?"

"No, *you* don't get it," Christie said. "Bend over and spread those skinny cheeks so I can get my hands on that Hello Kitty flash drive—"

Christie's eyes went wide. He toppled forward, and Jimmie crashed to the ground underneath the janitor's massive girth. Jimmie fought for air. He hadn't come this close to the end game to be smothered to death by a Dallas Cowboys fan. Jimmie summoned the power to roll Christie off of him just enough to slide out.

A machete was buried deep in Christie's back.

Jimmie snatched up the switchblade and spun around, looking for the assassin. The hallowed halls of the Lincoln Monument were empty of lurkers, though. He was the last man standing. Lincoln's somber visage stared across the carnage, disapproving but unable to do anything about it.

A closer look at the machete revealed an inscription, which read, "PROPERTY OF CARLY FIORINA." Apparently the former Hewlett-Packard CEO was cutting more than jobs now.

Jimmie's eyes flicked back to where Ted Cruz had been tied up. There was a pile of cut rope at the base of the pillar . . . and a deflated orca. Cruz and his oddball running mate Fiorina had absconded together, apparently. One of them had saved Jimmie from Christie, though, and he owed that person a debt of gratitude. Or possibly not. Maybe they could just call it even. Yeah, that sounded about right.

Jimmie limped over to Cat, who was just waking up. Sure, she'd planned to kill him. But she'd been acting on Trump's orders. At least that's what he told himself as he cut her free.

She fell into his arms. Her eyes fluttered open.

"I tried to kill you," she said.

"You weren't going to do it. I could tell all along, you weren't going to go through with it."

"I was, though. I had no reservations about—"

Jimmie placed a finger on her lips. "Shhhhh. You've been hit in the head pretty hard. Definitely a concussion. You don't know what you're saying."

"I was choked out," she said. "I never hit my head. I—"

"See? You don't even remember it. We'd better get you an MRI. Do you have a phone on you? I'll call the hospital—"

"You can use my helicopter," Trump interrupted. He was staggering toward them with Fiorina's bloody machete in one hand. "Except we won't be going to the hospital. I'll be taking you both to the morgue."

CHAPTER SIXTY-SIX

★ ★ ★ ★

GREAT AMERICA

Jimmie lowered Cat to the ground and stood guard in front of her. He waved the switchblade at Trump.

"Mine's bigger," the president said, pointing the blood-smeared tip of the machete at Jimmie, who had to admit that he was right. Trump had a full foot-long on him. But there was more to sword fighting than size. He hoped.

"Your janitor is dead," Jimmie said. "How do you expect to clean all this up?"

"I could just drop a bomb on this whole area. Wipe away the evidence with the push of a button. Wipe away DC with the push of a button."

"A nuke."

"It's actually not a button, did you know that?" Trump said. "All this talk in the campaign from people saying, 'Do we really want Trump's finger on the button?' And it's not a button! There are codes, there's a key. No button."

"You wouldn't do it."

Trump shook his head. "Not in a million years. But it's a nice thought. I prefer to keep my hands clean of dirty business like this . . . but you knew that I couldn't help myself from getting personally involved. Especially with the stakes. I had Corey tail you on Friday, when you left to see your ex. Using a microphone hidden in a salt shaker, he was able to listen to your entire conversation. He made a game-time decision to cut Emma from the game.

"Then he followed you back to the White House," Trump continued, "and you'll never guess what kind of trouble he saw you get up to."

Jimmie gulped.

"It was then that I decided you were a nuisance. I told the Navy SEALs I wanted you dead or alive. I specifically said, *If he accidentally gets shot in the face, it wouldn't be any sweat off my sack.* I show up at the museum, and there you are—still standing! Who knew that the Human Hiroshima had a code of honor? I left SEAL Team Sixty-Nine at home tonight. Some things are too big to trust others to do. If you want something done right . . ."

"You do it yourself," Jimmie finished. "Rule twelve, right?"

The switchblade trembled in Jimmie's hand as he backed up. He felt cold stone with his other palm. Out of the corner of his eye, he saw Cat crawling toward the gun that Trump had dropped. Was she going to use it on Trump . . . or on Jimmie? He would have to take his chances. And to do that, he was going to need to keep Trump talking.

"If you wouldn't drop a nuke on your own country," Jimmie said, stalling, "I'm going to guess you wouldn't risk starting World War III with the UK."

"You know, we kicked their ass twice—once in seventeen-whatever, then again in eighteen-whatever. It wouldn't be too hard to do it again. Usually, if you set up a best-of-three series and win the first two, you scrap the third one. Internal polling suggests the American people are all for it, though. But don't worry: I'm not going to war with England. I'm going to buy them out. It's a merger."

"The British people would never go for that."

Trump nodded. "Hence the threat of war. That's why they call it a hostile takeover. The queen won't get her bony ass off the throne. She's sitting on a gold mine of cash and jewels, which certain members of the royal family can't wait to get their hands on."

"Prince Charles?"

"That pussy? Puh-lease. Think further down the line, Jimmie," Trump said. "We're moving our ships into place as we speak. Before any shots are fired, England is going to wave the white flag. Great Britain and America are going to become one united country again: Great America. I'm going to be president still, of course. The Brits can keep their silly royal family. However, my first act will be to force the queen to hand her crown over . . . to Kate."

"Kate Middleton?"

Trump nodded. "We struck a deal. The prime minister and Parliament are in her pocket. The whole country loves her and her royal spawn. We ran into a minor snag with Hillary and Jeb!'s rebel alliance. Kate found out from British intelligence, who must have gotten word of it from Emma. Kate got cold feet—she said she'd call the deal off if I didn't clean up my own house. A hard body who plays hardball. I like her. Got a coupla kids, but she's a solid ten."

Jimmie shook his head. "Great America. *That's* what you meant by making America great again?"

"We're reshaping the world, Jimmie," Trump said. "Great America is going to be top dog. With England back in the fold, we're going to get a piece of that European economy— which will be incredibly strong, once we sell off Greece to the

Palestinians. Putin was going to bite off a piece of the European Union from the other side . . . but with him out of the way, Russia's no longer a player. If anyone wants to take us on for the title of biggest, baddest superpower, go for it. It'd be like showing up to a gun fight with a knife."

"Or a knife fight with a gun," Cat said, shooting the machete out of Trump's hand. It clattered to the ground several yards away. "Put your tiny hands above your head, Mr. President."

"Or what? You're going to shoot me?" Trump said, advancing toward her. "I was right about you illegals—just a bunch of murderers and—"

Another shot rang out, echoing through the monument's halls. At first, Jimmie thought she had missed Trump entirely. Then he noticed the tufts of wispy blond hair floating to the ground like cherry blossom leaves. She'd blown a hole the size of a fist in his famously unflappable mane. Trump held his palms out, desperately trying to catch the clumps of hair as they fell. He dropped to his hands and knees and began frantically scooping the rest into a pile.

CHAPTER SIXTY-SEVEN

★ ★ ★ ★

BIGGER THAN JESUS

"This is going to make quite the story," Cat said, watching Trump crying and rocking on the ground. "Too bad we're never going to be able to tell anybody."

"He thinks he's God," Jimmie said. "But he's just a man. A small man."

"I've got hands bigger than Jesus," Trump said from his knees. A river of golden tears streamed down his face. "Bigger than John Lennon. Bigger than Justin Bieber—"

"Don't say the Lord Bieber's name in vain," Jimmie snapped. Then to Cat, "Are you really an undocumented migrant?"

She stared daggers at him.

"Okay, okay—just asking," he said. "We can't let Trump get away with this. His plan to make America even greater needs to be exposed. Even if we can't tie him directly to any of the murders, he was about to kill us both."

"He was about to kill *you*. I think he would've let me go."

Jimmie said, "Sure. Whatever. My point is, there's enough evidence here to put him away for a long time."

She raised the gun at Jimmie.

"Whoa! What are you doing?" he said.

"If any of this gets out, I'll be put on trial for the murder of Lester Dorset," Cat said. "There's no way around it.

Even if the Secret Service did shoot him to death, I meant to kill him."

Jimmie had the switchblade in his hand still. If he moved fast enough, could he stab her in the hand with it and make her drop the gun?

"If we cover this up, the trail of bodies will only continue to grow," Jimmie said. "You could put a bullet in me . . . you could put one in Trump . . . but it won't end. I'm sorry. You may have killed Lester in a fit of rage—"

"It was a fit of passion," she said, trembling. "You know how passionate I get when breaking a story. I couldn't let him give the recordings away."

"I don't think that passion is for breaking a story—it's a passion for the truth. And it may be clouded by pageviews or viral shares and dreams of Pulitzers, but it's really about seeing the truth come to light."

"The truth is that I killed him over nothing," she said, the gun still trained on him. Her eyes were wet with tears. "You heard Trump."

"You had no idea the interviews were worthless. But it doesn't matter now. What matters is that we do the right thing."

"What do you suddenly know about doing the right thing?"

He shook his head. "Not much. But I'm learning."

She spun the gun around, and Jimmie took it by the handle. He breathed a sigh of relief. The switchblade thing would have never worked. It was like Christie had said: Writers had weak stabbing motions. Thankfully, it hadn't come to that—Cat had fallen for all that bullshit about the truth and doing the right thing. He'd been so convincing, he almost believed it himself.

In the distance, a single firework exploded in the sky near the National Monument. Then another, and another. Soon, they were being set off from all over the city. *Game of Thrones* had ended, and the people were rejoicing. Soon, they would flood the streets in ecstasy, overturning cars and setting them on fire. A great mob would form at the Lincoln Memorial and watch as the FBI led the president of the United States of America away in handcuffs.

"I'll be back," Trump would say, doing his best Arnold impersonation (which wouldn't be that bad). "I'm in the *Guinness Book of World Records* for the biggest financial comeback in history, you know. Someday, they're going to put me in for the biggest political comeback—you just watch, you bunch of losers!"

While the people would grudgingly accept the charges against him, their anger would fade over time, and they would one day accept the Donald back into their hearts, for there was nothing they loved more than a comeback story. And Jimmie Bernwood's comeback story was just beginning.

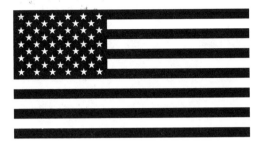

Three Months Later

EPILOGUE

★ ★ ★ ★

IN LOVING MEMORY

Jimmie stood before the bronze statue of Putin fighting the panda. He fingered the Pulitzer Prize ring on his pinkie. It hadn't solved all his problems, but it was a nice conversation starter on Tinder. They seemed less impressed with it on FarmersOnly.com.

Far behind him, Kate Middleton was droning on to the press corps about the greatness of America—the United States of America. The one and only America (unless you counted North America and South America, which nobody did).

To hear the Duchess of Cambridge tell it, there'd never been any deal on the table with Trump. She was clearly heeding the advice on the shirt Bill Clinton picked up at the Spy Museum gift shop: Deny everything. Though Trump liked to exaggerate, Jimmie had never known him to flat-out lie. There was some truth to what he'd said about the aborted geopolitical merger of the century. How much truth, nobody would ever know.

Regardless, World War III had been averted. Somebody sent Jimmie an SJW finch shirt as a thank-you. He'd donated it to Goodwill and saved the receipt for his taxes.

"He was an awful man," a familiar Eastern European voice said.

Jimmie turned around. At first, he thought Victoria Trump was talking about her estranged husband. He changed his mind when he saw her staring at Putin's bronzed visage. "I tried to tell Donny that Vladimir was evil. But Donny was always a sucker for anyone who goes hunting topless."

"I thought you'd already cleared out of here," Jimmie said.

She smiled warmly at him. "I left something behind."

He raised an eyebrow.

"I left you behind," she said, taking his hand. "I made a mistake. I told Donny about us. You could have been killed."

"It's not your fault. I should have taken you with me when I had the chance. What's done is done. We can't change the past—we can only change the future." He shook her off. "And my future isn't here. I'm leaving Washington."

Jimmie removed the lanyard from around his neck and dropped his badge at the base of the statue. It seemed like a fitting resting place: The memorial was on the same spot where Lester Dorset's body had been exhumed. The former first family's dachshund, Opulence, snatched up the lanyard and began tossing it around the South Lawn like a chew toy.

Victoria said, "But your job in the press corps—"

"My new editor at the *Daily Blabber* was just throwing me a bone," Jimmie said, shaking his head. "Everyone told me I'd be a fool not to accept the job, but that's what I am: a fool. I could give two shits about President Pedicab Ryan or politics in general."

"You broke the story on the Colonel Sanders. You were all over the news."

"You mean Bernie?" he said. After much digging, Jimmie had, indeed, found the former Democratic presidential candidate—in the Senate chamber. It was the same place Bernie had worked in virtual anonymity for years before the 2016 race and where he returned to following it. Though he'd been "missing" for over two years, no one had even thought to check the US Capitol Building for him.

Jimmie shook his head. "Sorry. This political stuff just doesn't do it for me. I was a fool to take this job."

"You are a very cute fool," Victoria said.

He took her in his arms and drew her close. The warmth of her body felt good against his. Her silicone was really heating up in the sun.

"I wish I could come with you, but there's another mistake I need to correct," he said. "The Zodiac Killer has struck again. I need to find Cruz."

She pouted. "Are you sure you can't . . . come with me?"

Behind her, a great bald eagle swooped down and plucked Opulence off the nine hole. Jimmie tried to refocus his gaze on Victoria, but he felt his eyes tracking upward as the dachshund was carried up and to the eagle's nest atop the Washington Monument.

She started to turn her head, but he planted his lips on the former first lady—partially to distract her and partially because he enjoyed kissing pretty girls.

They lapped at each other, needily, hungrily. The fact that she'd betrayed him faded with each long minute they stayed lip-locked. Jimmie was falling for her, all right. He hadn't thought he could feel like this about anyone after everything that had happened with Cat. It wasn't love, but it was close enough for government work.

Victoria broke away for air. "I need you right now, Mr. Jimmie. Let us find a restroom and make the love."

Jimmie was hard enough to cut a diamond but not desperate enough to get laid that he wanted to do it in a restroom. Plus, he had to get on the road—there was a killer out there. Then again . . . he could spare eight or nine minutes, couldn't he?

"Will your clearance level get us into the vice president's office, by any chance?" he asked, taking her hand. The VP, of course, was still in space. He'd be there a while. They'd accidentally launched him to Mars instead of the moon base.

Victoria nodded.

Biden's beanbag chair was going to need a good steam cleaning after today.

They raced hand in hand for the White House. Jimmie's conscience was mostly free—Victoria's divorce wasn't yet finalized, but her husband was behind bars. That's where Trump would remain for a good, long time. Thirty-two years, to be exact. Attempted murder and aggravated assault weren't cheap, as far as convictions went. Cat's sentence—life—was even harsher, but suffice to say Trump wouldn't be coming after Jimmie anytime soon.

However, it was a near certainty that the ex-president would be out long before his sentence was up. President Ryan wouldn't pardon him, but the next president might. And if they didn't, then another would. Someday, in their darkest hour, the American people would turn to the Donald and ask for his help making America great again (again)—again.

ABOUT THE AUTHOR

Andrew Shaffer is the *New York Times* best-selling author of *How to Survive a Sharknado and Other Unnatural Disasters*. His other works include the *Ghostbusters* tie-in *Ghosts from Our Past* and *Fifty Shames of Earl Grey: A Parody*. Shaffer and his work have been featured on *The Colbert Report*, NPR, Fox News's *Fox and Friends*, CBS's *The Early Show, Mental Floss*, and *Maxim*. This is his first thriller.

ACKNOWLEDGMENTS

I would like to thank editor Anne Brewer, publisher Matt Martz, publicists Dana Kaye and Julia Borcherts, and the rest of the staff at Crooked Lane Books. You were a pleasure to work with.

I would like to thank my agent, Brandi Bowles, at Foundry Literary + Media.

I would like to thank Tiffany Reisz, Jenn LeBlanc, and Keegan Murphy for listening to me ramble and for rambling right back.

And lastly, I would like to thank Donald J. Trump for making politics great again.